Arnold Jansen op de Haar

King of Tuzla

Translated by Paul Vincent

Arnold

Holland Park Press London

First published by Holland Park Press 2010
Updated version published by Holland Park Press 2011

Copyright © Arnold Jansen op de Haar 2010
English translation © Paul Vincent 2010

First published in The Netherlands as *De koning van Tuzla* by De Arbeiderspers 1999

The moral right of Arnold Jansen op de Haar to be identified as the author of this work has been asserted by him in accordance with the Copyright, Designs and Patents Act of 1988.

All rights reserved. Without limiting the rights under the copyright reserved above, no part of this publication may be reproduced, stored in a retrieval system or transmitted in any form or by any means, electronic, mechanical, photocopying, recording or otherwise, without the prior permission of both the copyright owner and Holland Park Press.

A CIP catalogue record for this book is available from The British Library.

ISBN 978-1-907320-06-4

Cover designed by Reactive Graphics

Printed and bound in Great Britain by
CPI Antony Rowe, Chippenham and Eastbourne

www.hollandparkpress.co.uk

All of a sudden Tijmen Klein Gildekamp, a young army captain, finds himself in a real war. He is part of the UN, based in Bosnia in the former Yugoslavia, the scene of the most recent war in Europe.

King of Tuzla is not so much about military battles or strategies rather it focuses on how war affects ordinary people, both soldiers and civilians.

Interspersed with Tijmen's story about finding his own identity within a strict military environment, we are shown vivid snippets of life in the war zone:

> Civil servant Galib Prolaz, a self proclaimed Yugoslavian citizen who, after the Muslims were driven away, had no alternative but to become a farmer.

> The beautiful Lucia Mezga, who behind the bar of 'Holland House', dreams that officers are queuing up to marry her.

Do Tijmen's ambitions survive this war? Does he come to terms with how he has changed?

King of Tuzla is a truly original coming-of-age story.

Personne n'avait vu l'homme se noyer que moi.
　Marguerite Duras

*I was much further out than you thought
And not waving but drowning.*
　Stevie Smith

CONTENTS

Part I   11
Double Game

Part II   73
Interbellum

Part III   101
A Smell of War

Part IV   133
Dancing on a Cold Tiled Floor

Part V   171
An Evening in Simin Han

PART I
DOUBLE GAME

In the snow-covered wood above the road old Galib Prolaz, 'the Yugoslav', like a sleepwalker, was chopping timber into small blocks that he would later take home. Propped against his wheelbarrow was his hunting rifle, an heirloom from his father, who under Tito had used it to fight the Germans.

Galib had a wife, Raza, and two daughters: Svetlana, named after Stalin's daughter, and Fata. Both were still unmarried, although they were well over thirty. This caused resentful gossip among the villagers, and behind Galib's back they said he thought he was too good for them. Sometimes he heard the whispering behind him. But he had little to do with the village: his house was on the edge of it, in a plum orchard. Only on Fridays did he go down to the village to attend the mosque.

When the first rumours of night-time massacres reached the village, he had stubbornly denied them; he was a Yugoslav and would always remain one. Every morning his wife still made his sandwiches and he went cheerfully to the town hall, where he worked in the registry.

The bullying had started almost imperceptibly. At times his papers would go missing, at others someone would have moved his desk. During lunch his table became increasingly empty. He was blamed for the disappearance of three blank passports, which, as everyone knew, fetched a fortune on the black market. After that Galib had the table to himself. But they didn't dare fire him, though less and less work landed on his desk.

Till one morning it proved impossible to travel to town. The Muslims had been driven out of their homes in the night. At least, that was what Alija, Hamzić's son, had told him on the way. Galib had returned home with his briefcase and his sandwiches. He said to his wife that it really was war now.

Not long after, in his own village, 'the man from Marrakech' had disappeared; he was blue like the men who lived in the southern Atlas Mountains. No one knew his name or where exactly he came from. 'Marrakech', he would say with a vague smile when asked. He'd appeared in the village one day and had never left. He lived on what people gave him and led an unobtrusive life, until his sudden disappearance. The man from Marrakech sparked a panic. The following night all the Croats had head over heels to leave the village.

Since then Galib had worked on his vegetable plot, cut wood and fetched water from the stream. Fortunately, he still had a couple of goats that gave plenty of milk. He had always bred goats in his spare time. He even won prizes with them, but he had never thought they would come in handy like this. What he had always tried to prevent had happened after all: he, the proud civil servant Galib Prolaz, the Yugoslav, had become a farmer among farmers.

For a while he drank rakija with the men of the village. His pride seemed finally to have been broken. But when they started saying that all Croats were 'Ustašas', and what they'd do if they got hold of one, he'd got up, upturned the table and sent the cards flying through the bar. The bar owner had tried to throw him out, but Galib had warded him off with his strong hands and shouted: 'I'll always be the Yugoslav.'

'Dangerous words,' said the mullah later.

After that Galib withdrew into his house and lived on what the poor land provided. At the beginning of winter he had sold his train collection. In that way he hoped to survive to the end of the war, although he could feel the strength slowly flowing out of his body. If he had not been taking care of his wife and daughters, he would long since have lost heart.

He chopped doggedly on. There was snow in the air. Just one more day and then he wouldn't need to come out for a while.

The faint hum of the car engine shut out all other sound. Three more weeks and it would be Christmas. Tijmen was afraid. It wasn't the fear he'd once felt in downtown San Francisco, when he was threatened by three huge black guys with flashing knives. This fear was more deep-seated, in his head, elusive. Normally speaking, he would be about a third of the way through his life now. At least as far as you could talk about normal expectations in this crap country.

It was the same fear he had felt last night, far from home, in streets he didn't know, full of ghostly figures who passed you by without a nod.

In the darkness convoys of trucks had thundered past, he remembered. There seemed to be more of them than during the day. From one of the houses came the sound of the last melancholy notes of Rachmaninov's Second Piano Concerto. The lights were still on in a bar; a drunken soldier stumbled out, saw him and launched into the Horst-Wessel Lied. Tijmen had done an about-turn. He yelled at the mountains: 'I'm coming!' His loud voice pierced the deep silence. Further down, the streetlights came on and on an upper floor someone opened the shutters.

When he got back to the hotel all the lights had been turned off. In his room there was no sound but the snoring of Lex under the sheets. He hadn't switched the light on, but groped his way to bed.

Tijmen Klein Gildekamp, commander of Alpha Company, shared the car with his colleagues from Bravo and Charlie, Eddy and Lex. He, Eddy and Lex all had the same rank, captain, and similar jobs. What's more, they all seemed to be about the same height. None of the three was as tall as grenadiers once used to be.

Although he was two years older than Lex, Eddy had an open, round, almost childlike face. Lex, on the other hand, had sharp features that could easily be interpreted as vicious. For Eddy war was a game, for Lex every game was a war in itself. Tijmen surveyed his colleagues and felt warm sympathy welling up in him. Back then, in December 1993, he still regarded both of them as 'best mates'.

The string of white vehicles, seven in all, followed at high speed the lead car with the three company commanders in it: the 'young bloods' or 'gang of three', as the battalion's Commanding Officer Verbeek called them. Verbeek in turn was dubbed 'the old man' by them. The old man, who travelled with the deputy brigade commander, drove in the second car, and they were followed by a number of officers from the Army Ordnance Corps. Then came the cars of the doctor and the officers from the helicopter detachment and finally two vehicles containing battalion administrative staff. All of them were equipped with a blue Kevlar helmet, a flak jacket in camouflage colours and a pistol, which had been issued at the logistical base in Split. This must have been a strange sight for the local police, since only commanders carried pistols in these parts: 'many chiefs, no Indians'.

It was the Dutchbat reconnaissance party tearing down the road. The reconnaissance team of the battalion which, for so long, had been disappointed about the mission to Cambodia that had been called off. They had had to wait for over a year but now the new task in Bosnia beckoned: a real war.

During their stay in Croatia there had not as yet been much sign of that war, even though the children by the roadside stuck up their middle fingers at them and once even threw stones. If you wanted to go out for a walk from the Palace Hotel in Trogir, you had to be in civvies, and when the bouncers in nearby Split realised they were dealing with UN soldiers, they refused you entry. Finally Tijmen, Lex and Eddy were beckoned into a back alley, far from the bustle downtown, by two men in long leather coats. Their German marks were exchanged for a pile of useless Croatian banknotes.

'Hey, skull,' cried Lex to Tijmen from the back of the car, 'at last we've seen the last of that shit hotel.'

They had spent two nights in the Palace.

'You never know how long Croat permission to leave will take,' the commander of the Dutch logistical base had said to

Tijmen, 'certainly not now a Dutch sergeant-major has just smuggled two Bosnian women out of the country.'

The major, still young, had made an impression on him of nervousness. The Croatian authorities had been threatening for weeks to terminate the lease of the complex and at the weekend a ban had been announced on any UN movement. 'Because of the tourism' was the official explanation, which seemed mainly intended to stall the UN.

Yet their stay in the Palace had been limited to those two days. It was a hotel that exuded decay on all sides. The white paint on the sea-facing veranda was flaking off here and there, most bulbs were missing from the chandeliers on the ceiling and the breakfast consisted of not much more than baguettes and an indefinable substance with the taste of cat food squashed onto a grubby plate. All was served with a mug of warm milk with a thick skin floating in it. The cellar of the hotel had been transformed into a restaurant where pizza, rice and chips could be eaten for hard currency.

The marble lobby of the hotel was the assembly point for the military. They were always cheerful, because they were being allowed home, or 'up there', as everyone called it, to Bosnia.

In the weak winter sunshine the Kaštelanski Zaljev, the 'bay of castles' (once built as a defence against the Turks), had looked like the English seaside on a Monday morning: completely deserted. Two kilometres away was the walled town of Trogir, a little harbour of the kind you find all over the Adriatic. It was a pretty town, with its reliefs, cornices and loggias in shifting shades, old buildings with Greek and Venetian statuary, meandering alleyways, colourful fishing boats in the harbour, a promenade with shady trees, yellow palms and a whole row of terraces. It was never really winter here. In this place you saw men kissing one another in greeting, and young people on scooters gathering in the market square; you heard unintelligible sounds (but be sure not to call them 'Yugoslav'); there were small cups of Turkish coffee (but don't call it 'Turkish coffee') with slivovitz, at eight-thirty in the morning; and then the old men with steaming loaves under their arms; on the sights signs saying 'zatvoren', closed, and in the afternoons the roller blinds on the shop fronts were down; the macho types in sunglasses separate from the women chatting in groups; the bright-red roofs; the half-built concrete skeletons put up by developers and speculators; and the respect for the authorities in tall black caps. It was, in short, the Adriatic, only as it was twenty years ago.

There were no tourists now. The postcards showing crowded beaches and the resort's hotels were the only reminder of the Yugoslavia of the travel guides, cheap flights and package tours. Almost every balcony was obscured by washing lines covered in flapping garments, in motley of military camouflage gear and the disintegrating clothes of refugees.

The people in Trogir were nicer than those in Split. UNPROFOR was an important source of income. But the arrival of groups of soldiers from 'particular countries' with their own 'particular' habits threatened to disrupt relations. The soldiers from those countries, who had been away from home for months, sometimes walked hand in hand along the beach and two of them had been arrested for the rape of a little boy who was playing near their hotel.

The arrival of the Croatian girls' volleyball team created some excitement on the last evening in the hotel. Tijmen had wondered how on earth it was possible they were staying in a UN hotel. Asking the girls had proved impossible since they were accompanied by broad-shouldered men who forbade any approach.

Actually Tijmen was very shy about those sorts of things. It was not without reason that Lex often asked him how often he did it. And when Tijmen asked, 'What do you mean?' Lex would shout: 'You know, without pussy.'

Tijmen was a loner. No one must get too close to him. In relationships with women he felt powerless. The idea he once had that his military career would change everything, now struck him as a bad joke.

'Bloody hell, if it goes on like this I might as well trade in my kidneys!'

Lex was curled up among the luggage. When the battalion reconnaissance party left Split, it had been his lot to sit at the back among the anti-shrapnel blankets, Eddy was at the wheel, and Tijmen sat next to him with the map.

The first part of the route was on the well-maintained roads along the coast. The area resembled the arid landscape of California, Tijmen thought. Gently rolling rocky hills covered with prickly undergrowth, and on the southern slopes, growing among the boulders, olive trees and long rows of vines. For kilometres the cars drove in the shadow of the cliffs that separated the coastal strip from the hinterland: a virtually impregnable wall of rock hundreds of metres high. Slowly the olive trees and vines also disappeared. After the convoy left the Dalmatian coast through a gateway in the wall, a steep pass, the landscape became grimmer and the season changed in a trice: from full-colour to black-and-white. The roads soon turned into muddy tracks, and the black earth sucked at the tyres.

There was enough time to read during the reconnaissance, but Tijmen didn't read. For now his books remained untouched in his pack. He had once turned the conversation to literature, but that didn't go down too well with the others.

Eddy cheerfully struck up a song. He whistled a simple tune, loudly and off-key, 'It's a long way to Tipperary...', a marching song. This was his finest hour, war at last. He was proud, thought Tijmen. You could see that at a glance. Perhaps as proud as he himself.

Eddy read too, as long as it was about the Second World War. He knew everything there was to know about the Battle of Arnhem. With the men of his company he had regularly retraced the three routes of the advance: below along the Rhine, along the railway through the centre of town, and past the spot where the attack had become bogged down at the Leeren Doedel restaurant. Behind the building, which now housed a pizzeria, you could still see the outlines of the foxholes. He regularly crossed the battlefield accompanied by the chain-smoking 'official battlefield guide'– a British sergeant who had stayed on in Oosterbeek after the war and was to be found every day at the village's war cemetery. The exact location of the tree in which the initials of the Hohenstaufen division had been carved, the wood next to the mental asylum in Wolfheze, where the British reconnaissance party had been cut to pieces by an ss company ('they didn't even have time to get out of their gliders – they may have been betrayed'), the company headquarters at Utrechtseweg 222 – he knew them all. Eddy had shown Tijmen the mutilated trees near Mill Hill in Oosterbeek from which you could still see, fifty years on, how the British had walked into an ambush. In the places where bullets had struck the wood, strange protuberances grew from the trees like rampant boils.

It went quiet in the car when they stopped at a border checkpoint manned by dour Croat police. Over the radio came the colonel's voice ordering them to put on their flak jackets and have their helmets ready. The policeman took a cursory look in the vehicles and motioned a colleague to check their papers.

Shortly after, the vehicles were climbing at walking pace up a winding road. They stopped briefly to fit snow chains to the tyres. Lex helped the old man, who, with a big cigar in his mouth, watched the captain at work.

Before them lay the rugged, mountainous landscape of Bosnia, with its virtually impassable rivers, the Bosna, Miljacka and Neretva, the bridges in ruins and roads mined.

Eddy steered the vehicle through a deep pothole.

'Panti Nikkainen, the Finnish rally ace!' yelled Lex.

At the side of the road three women with great piles of firewood on their backs slowed down to let the vehicles pass. It had struck Tijmen previously that women seemed to do all the heavy work around here. They stared at him with expressionless faces. Here they had been used to foreign warlords for centuries.

'Nice babe!' cried Eddy.

'This is what you call nice babe,' retorted Lex, and slapped the December playmate against the back windscreen. Eddy sprayed the screen clean. Tijmen could see in his mirror that the vehicle behind them was getting dangerously close. The colonel hung out of the window and gave them an enthusiastic thumbs-up.

'Let's lose the old man,' cried Eddy.

'Go, go, go!' yelled Lex.

The car alternately skidded on the bends, and creaked with the strain on the shock-absorbers when they hit a pothole.

'Go, go, go!'

Suddenly there was an unexpected movement. The car spun on its own axis, there was yelling, then an abrupt halt. From the second vehicle the colonel warned them to take it easy.

'Panti Nikkainen,' laughed Lex.

Eddy's neck went deep red and he turned round.

'Will you put a sock in it?'

Since the previous evening something had been brewing. Once, when drunk, Eddy had confided to the others what he found the biggest turn-on. 'And I always pull her plaits,' he had added.

Every time they passed a girl after that Lex would yell: 'Look Eddy, plaits!' giving him a dig in the back.

Tijmen had listened as if he wasn't one of them. But, since military academy, he definitely was one of them, even though they weren't then yet a 'gang of three'. Eddy was a year ahead of him and Lex a year behind. And you didn't mix with those years. Even years were 'good years', odd years on the other hand were 'shit years'. And when he was elected to the Senate of the Cadet Corps at the end of the second year, Tijmen felt superior even to his own year; during initiation the new recruits had had to call out 'respect' when he went past.

Originally he had happily gone to the academy of his own free will. His parents were amazed at his carefree attitude, but in fact when he arrived he was astonished by the world he found. It had been a failed attempt to give shape to his life, and only his stubbornness prevented him from giving up. At the end of the second year the senate beckoned. The senate was his Parnassus. That year was an idyll. In the company of his fellow-senators he *was* someone, he felt strong. That feeling of empowerment had never fully returned.

Respect for the senate! Laughable, putting on airs like that. Nowadays, he scarcely mentioned it any more. Certainly not since he had become a red beret, and not when the beret had become blue. And yet, when he looked back he still felt a certain pride. He hadn't seen the senators for years. 'Illustrious Ones', the ex-senators were called. David was the only one he still saw occasionally.

At the back of the car Lex opened the emergency rations with his pocket knife. He spread pâté on the biscuits. He gave one to Eddy. Then he hunted in his breast pocket and asked for a cigarette,

'On the cadge,' said Eddy, but he was laughing.

No one could be angry with Lex for long. He was the typical tough guy, already popular at the academy, and he belonged to the 'rowing fraternity'. Lex was the star of the annual cabaret, and no one was better at playing himself, playing *them*.

The cadets in the audience had roared with laughter.

'Ministry of Defence,' said the girl.

'Where is the bomb?' asked the deep voice.

Lex read out the bomb report form in its entirety. He could have chosen any army form: the audience was eating out of his hand.

'I'll put you through.'

'Where is the bomb?' and he rattled off the list of questions again.

From the poster hanging beside the stage Uncle Sam thrust his finger at the audience. 'THE CORPS NEEDS YOU' it said in large letters underneath.

The gales of laughter in the auditorium had sounded like gunfire.

The day before Lex had performed a wonderful sketch about a Spanish officer. ('Mucho placer a la barricada: have fun on the obstacle course.') It was just that Tijmen found it difficult to take when Lex sent *him* up.

The convoy wasn't making much headway. Several times the vehicles had to stop to let oncoming traffic pass. Not until late afternoon did they reach Tomislavgrad. The map called it 'Duvno'.

Tijmen exchanged a few words with a Croat soldier and asked if Tomislav was a Yugoslav name. The man turned away with a look of disgust.

'That's right,' said Eddy, 'according to me he's a Croat warlord from the tenth century.'

'There's a snowstorm on the way,' said the British by the roadside, and further on the road was blocked by the snowed-in vehicles of Solidarité, a French aid organisation. A snow plough was clearing a way north, like a big black slug.

The colonel appeared at the lead vehicle and tapped on the window. 'We're staying in the British camp tonight,' said his lips.

Tijmen dragged his rucksack to the cold gym. The apparatus stood there unused. The bronze bust of Tito stared down at Tijmen from the stage – he was still on a pedestal here. At the great leader's funeral a million people had stood by the railway tracks as the train carrying his remains passed, but now Tito had been banished to back rooms. A French convoy had got stuck here a few hours earlier, and a few of the legionnaires were already asleep. Lex called their thin sleeping bags 'cigarette papers'. The colonel of the brigade staff had made himself comfortable and was enjoying a beer as he read a tabloid. When he saw Tijmen he indicated the breasts of the page-three girl with a wide grin.

All day long Tijmen had eaten nothing but a few biscuits. When the greasy smell of an English meal penetrated the dormitory, his stomach rumbled. The smell of baked beans and offal. Outside the wind that they called the 'bora' whistled its treacherous lullaby.

The next morning Tijmen woke from a light sleep. The room he was in was pitch-black. There was a penetrating smell of sweat and stale beer. On both sides he felt warm bodies turning in their sleep. It was some minutes before he realised where he was: slow, black minutes in which his breath stopped short. He needed to take a leak but decided to hold it in. Finding his way in the dark between the sleeping bodies was not very appealing.

When he woke a few hours later the light was on. It was a quarter past seven. The wind had created frost flowers on the window panes. Some of the sleeping bags were empty, but the colonel still lay there snoring.

In the dimly-lit washroom Tijmen looked at his face. The bags under his eyes were getting darker and darker.

It was busy in the mess. The soldiers in the stranded convoys wanted to get to their destinations as quickly as possible. The same baked beans as had been served the night before, this time with long strips of fried bacon.

Once, ages ago, this had been the world he wanted to belong to. Now he was part of it with his whole being. In Holland a hundred and thirty soldiers were awaiting his return. Just as the colonel was 'the old man' to his company commanders, so Tijmen was the old man to his men.

Outside the wind had dropped, and it was a clear day. Eddy was scraping the ice off the front windscreen and Lex, looking around cautiously, lugged a package wrapped in a blanket into the vehicle.

During the night the wind had blown drifts of snow against the cars and Tijmen dug the tyres free with a big shovel. After checking their weapons and UN IDs the convoy set off, again with the company commanders' car in the lead. The snow, metres deep, made the road almost invisible, and only the sawn-off electricity poles by the roadside and sometimes a bridge indicated the route.

They had scarcely got moving before a black Mercedes loomed up in the distance. Since the Croat offensive the area had been full of irregular troops. The car approached swinging from side to side like a drunk leaving the pub. At the sides it was reinforced with thick plates of steel and the bonnet boasted two human skulls. The driver was hanging out of the window, hair blowing in the wind. As he passed he raised two fingers provocatively. Eddy waved back cheerfully.

The 'goat track' through the mountains built by British engineers was unmistakable. On the right, close to the track was a yawning precipice, and even closer, on the left, the bare cliffs towered high above the vehicles. The British tried to regulate the traffic as well as they could. Vehicles could not pass each other, and this was the only access to Central Bosnia. The goat track was occupied in turn by aid convoys, blue helmets and the Croat offensive.

Almost all the Zastavas, Wartburgs and Yugos carried number plates bearing the letters 'HVO' of the Bosnian-Croatian army. Eddy zigzagged cautiously between unshaven, tired-looking soldiers. Profiteers, waiting patiently in run-down caravans, interrupted their games of cards to sell their goods or watery soup to the passing convoys. They passed a ravine with an overturned tanker in it, scorched black, with the letters 'UN' still just legible.

The sun broke through. Down below the half frozen Lake Prozor glistened. The map gave its real name as Ramsko jezero. 'Too difficult,' decided Eddy and dubbed it 'the lake of Prozor'. The road wound its way for kilometres along the cliff wall. As if on a Christmas card, new vistas across the water opened up at every bend.

The convoy stopped at a British checkpoint for lunch and the men got out. Tijmen screwed up his eyes. In the middle of the lake was an island with a large building on it. Its roof glittered in the sun. Behind him Tijmen could hear the clicking of cameras. He half-turned, put his right foot on a stone and stuck his chin in the air: the pose of a commander.

It was only much later, when the photos were developed that he saw that Lex had stuck up two fingers behind his head.

An hour later the convoy temporarily left the goat track. In the distance there were houses clinging to a mountainside. There were few signs that only two months before a great Croat offensive had taken place. 'Twenty thousand men', the papers had said.

Over the radio came a message telling them to drive 'nose-to-tail', as protection against the population of Prozor, who had built wooden steps by the side of the road to make it easier to steal goods from the vehicles. Large black crosses had been painted on the doors of undamaged, freshly whitewashed Croat houses. The remaining houses in Prozor had been gutted and slogans had been painted on their windowless walls, signed 'HDZ': this arm of the Croatian Democratic Union reached deep into Bosnia. Household effects were scattered through gardens. Tijmen saw a toy bear sticking out of the snow like a limbless trunk.

In Gornji Vakuf the convoy acquired an escort of two British armoured personnel carriers and the vehicles drove twisting and turning past deep craters in the road. Virtually all the houses were damaged. The people were shrouded in rags, shelves in shops empty, and the streets filled with the smell of burnt flesh. A stream constituted the front line, and on either side there were trenches, on one side manned by Croat troops and on the other by Muslim fighters. The front line was frozen over, as it was every winter. Not until the spring would the conflict flare up again.

Tijmen and Eddy looked at each other.

'Christ, man, what a stink,' Eddy called to the back.

'It's not me,' shouted Lex.

'It *is* you.'

'OK, OK,' Lex admitted after some further insistence, 'my insides are completely rotten.'

He burped loudly and the men laughed.

And you should have heard his answering machine. Just as Eddy's machine always played the Grenadiers' March first, Lex's message was: 'If you really need to burp, do so after the beep.'

Tijmen regarded Lex with a mixture of aversion and admiration. Being so intelligent and yet living the way he did, without ever-recurring doubt, must make things easy. Nonchalant, a woman chaser when he felt like it – 'tarts, lonely hearts and taxis' as Lex called it – and with a certain low cunning... He was going to make it big one day. And what about himself, Tijmen? For other people he was just like Eddy and Lex. No one knew who he was. He didn't even know himself.

His reflections were rudely interrupted by Eddy, as the convoy passed a bridge. From the trenches on either side of the river the waving arms of the Muslim fighters and their Croat opponents stuck out above ground level.

In the summer months the Muslims and Croats had been involved in barbaric hand-to-hand combat. In the north the Bosnian Serbs, lacking infantry, had made ample use of artillery and mortars, but now, in winter, the whole country was in the grip of an iron stalemate.

The British had been bold enough to set up camp in a brand new flour mill on the edge of the village. Tijmen consulted his guide book. The only local sight mentioned was the mountain scenery around Gornji Vakuf and the memorial to the battle of Neretva (1943). Eddy said that Tito had conducted negotiations with the Germans in Gornji Vakuf. They had almost reached an agreement, when a message arrived from Berlin instructing the German negotiators to break off contact with Tito: there was no question of negotiating with 'rebels'.

After Gornji Vakuf came the most dangerous part of the route: a bumpy road through a ravine many kilometres long by a fast-flowing river. The mujahideen were active here. A week before a Dutch convoy of the transport battalion had come under fire; later the Dutchmen would proudly show the dents in their flak jackets.

The wheels of the vehicles slipped and slid across the icy road, while the jagged boulders regularly came dangerously close. At the back of the vehicle the bust of Tito shook to and fro, adorned with an orange T-shirt. The snow hung heavily on the branches of the conifers. By the side of the road a trail of footsteps went uphill.

Tijmen scanned the slopes. He could see no ambushes, nor hear any gunfire or explosions, only an icy silence. The summit was shrouded in shreds of mist. Every kilometre the danger became more oppressive, but each was another gain. Two Dutch military policemen were supposed to have been robbed of their vehicle around here. After a few tricky moments, when the men were pushed face down in the snow, they had had to walk the whole stretch back to Gornji Vakuf.

Tijmen felt as if he were being slowly sucked towards danger. He felt a kind of exhilarating fear. Thank God he was no longer somewhere on the periphery of society, but where it was all happening: in the spotlight. Action at last.

Galib Prolaz had almost filled his wheelbarrow. He had not been able to finish the job yesterday, but if he carried on working for a little longer now, he wouldn't have to come out again for a while. He had resigned himself to the loss of his job with the council. It took more than that to break him, Galib. He swore under his breath.

Still every day more refugees arrived in the village. Together with the new residents had come rumours of a permanent truce between Muslims and Croats. Galib scarcely dared believe them. There had been talk of a ceasefire before, but every failed attempt meant even more bitter fighting.

The house next to Galib's place had stood empty for a year. His former neighbour had fled to Germany. For thirty years Dragan had dropped by every evening after work, and eaten with the family. Dragan was more than a neighbour, he was a friend. Dragan, who played his harmonica for them. Dragan, with whom he went fishing in the river every Saturday. His household effects had been divided up among the villagers.

He had spoken to his new neighbours, the Hasanović family, for the first time yesterday. Murat, the grandfather, had introduced his daughter and daughter-in-law, and their four children. They came from the area between Banja Luka and Prijedor. They were frightened people, reluctant to trouble anyone.

Galib grabbed a new trunk. He had finished his own pile, but he didn't want to go home yet. Murat would be bound to have use for a small supply of wood.

Murat had told him, in a soft voice, how they had been driven from their home, how the soldiers had interrogated his son and son-in-law while they all stood there. Then they were taken away. He hadn't even been able to say goodbye. The women were also interrogated, separately. He wouldn't say anything about that. Then they had been given a quarter of an hour to gather together their possessions. He had just packed whatever was to hand. They were driven onto the trucks by the soldiers. There wasn't enough room for so many people. As they drove off they had just managed to see their house being set on fire: the house Murat had worked all his life for.

Murat had talked of the Serb 'St Peter's Day fires on 11 July', the road of death to Banja Luka; about the corpses at the roadside, the blackened houses. The Hasanović family had had a long journey from one refugee camp to another, from one gym to another full of shivering people. For months they had slept in those kinds of emergency centres. If you were lucky, you were able to get hold of a bunk bed. That offered a little privacy, since you could make a curtain of the blanket. They had inquired everywhere about the fate of their menfolk but had received no reply. All they were told was that the Puharska mosque in Prijedor had also been blown up. Murat had pinned the names of his loved ones on every notice board, together with their photos, and had filled in countless forms for the Red Cross.

In the valley Galib heard the growl of a column of vehicles. There was no time to disappear over the top of the hill. He crouched down hurriedly behind a pile of wood. He grabbed his weapon, pulled the butt into his shoulder, with the barrel pointing at the bend in the road. The sound came closer. He held his breath. His finger curled round the trigger.

Suddenly the first vehicle appeared. Galib narrowed his eyes. He sighed and lowered his rifle, his arms limp at his sides. The white vehicles carried the 'UN' sign in large black letters.

The cars stopped and men got out, laughing and throwing snowballs. Their voices sounded muted: every sound was muffled by the snow. They pissed in the verge, and it made yellow circles in the pristine landscape.

He waited until they had gone and only when the last tail-lights had disappeared, did he get up and rub his stiff limbs. He piled the rest of the wood onto his wheelbarrow and Galib Prolaz, the Yugoslav, walked slowly to his house in the plum orchard, which now lay desolate and deserted.

The ravine widened and the convoy gathered speed. A long line of men with hunting rifles on their shoulders were jogging through a field to an unspecified destination. At the back was a fighter with a brand-new Dragunov sniper's rifle. Eddy took more photos.

Many houses at the roadside consisted of a single-storey ground floor in concrete. That had little connection with the war. As in many Southern regions people here built their own houses: first the ground floor, and if more money was available a first, and sometimes a second floor would follow.

In the Muslim villages women and children stood by the roadside, waving and begging for food, sweets and cigarettes. A hairpin bend – where the people knew the convoys had to brake – was lined with old men, mothers in Turkish harem trousers and colourful headscarves, lifting up their children, the cheekiest of whom pointed to their mouths and tummies. In Split, Tijmen had been given express instructions not to give away anything en route; it wouldn't be the first time that children had been run over by vehicles thundering past. Lex steered at walking pace through the howling throng. He was doing his stint of driving.

'The guys in the transport battalion call this "Bombon Alley",' said Eddy.

When the begging children realised they would get nothing from the Dutch, they pelted the departing vehicles furiously with stones.

By the time the convoy reached the Croat 'pocket' surrounded by Muslim fighters the men felt shattered. The mountains were behind them. The snow had suddenly vanished, as if the landscape were finally surrendering. It was drizzling.

From a long way off Tijmen could see the red-and-white checked flags, and the banners with anti-UN slogans. For the first time since the convoy had set foot on Bosnian soil, they were back on an asphalted road. Most people in the street ignored the vehicles; the odd person, with a furious look, stuck two fingers in the air. At a crossroads near Novi Travnik two burnt-out buses stood there like dinosaur skeletons, their tyres stolen and there were dark stains on the asphalt. Eddy pointed at them.

'Look,' he said, 'that's what's left of the *Convoy for Peace* that tried to make it to Tuzla this spring. In Novi Travnik the convoy was attacked by furious Croats. Saw it on the BBC. If you'd like to see it, I've got the documentary on tape.'

Eddy had everything 'on tape'. The silence in the car was broken only by his comments or the clicking of his camera. He was looking around with the almost frightening rapture of an overexcited child.

Lex drove the car at high speed over the wet asphalt. To the right was the camp belonging to Bravo Company of the transport battalion in Šantići. Lex pointed to the abandoned houses on a hill to the left: a ghost town with walls scorched black as silent witnesses of 'ethnic cleansing'. That must have been quite some time ago, because all the household effects had disappeared. Eddy again tried to take photographs.

A quarter of an hour later the vehicle drove into the headquarters of the Belgo-Dutch transport battalion in Busovača. Lex joked about the long-haired soldiers at the gate, distributing sweets to the screaming children. Immediately on arrival the guests were received in the hotel, which had been transformed into the staff headquarters of the transport battalion, a wooden building that looked like a Swiss chalet, with cheerful red and white checked curtains.

The commander greeted his guests excitedly, and then suggested a guided tour. He pointed proudly to the swimming pool that was being built and was due to be finished by spring.

The water supply in the camp still left a lot to be desired: the local council no longer had reliable information about the water network. They had finally found the location where a well could be sunk on old SS topographic maps. Then the newcomers were shown the tennis court and the gym. In his enthusiasm the Dutch commander stumbled over his words. He said, 'In two months I've achieved more than my predecessor did in his whole deployment.'

At the end of their tour of the camp they were shown to their quarters under canvas. Meanwhile the commander had been called away. Someone had scrawled in large letters on the tent: 'AIRMOBILE BRIGADE GO HOME'.

Outside it was drizzly winter weather and the atmosphere in the bar was as stuffy as a truck stop. The music pounding out of the speakers made conversation virtually impossible. Every five minutes the 'pizza song' was turned up to full volume.

'Sloeters, her name was,' yelled Eddy over the din, 'Chantal Sloeters.'

One foundation day Sloeters had been elected 'the ugliest man at the Royal Military Academy'. It had been an open election, won fair and square by Miss Chantal Sloeters. After all, Chantal Sloeters did have a moustache, and the objectionable habit of lying in wait, dressed in nothing but a pair of panties, for some cadet to return from town smashed out of his head. She would then force her way into the unfortunate guy's quarters and pounce on her victim.

Eddy pointed to the female chaplain.

'Sloeters was uglier,' said Lex,

Niki, the chaplain, saw the men looking at her and came over to them.

The colonel had come in and the volume control was turned down.

'You lot aren't talking about me, are you?' asked Niki.

'No,' said Lex, 'nothing special, old stories from the academy, beautiful.'

'Yes,' said Tijmen. 'Do you remember Adri, the caretaker?'

The men sniggered.

'Adri was the surly caretaker of one of the blocks,' Tijmen began.

'PBP block,' said Eddy.

'Listen... so Adri, this caretaker, was rung up one evening from the fourth floor and told that the handlebars of a bike had been found. "We'll send them down in the lift," said the voice. "Can you just chuck it in the skip?" Adri threw it good-humouredly into the skip and a little later did the same with the saddle, the wheels and the luggage rack, which came down in the lift one after the other. The guy spent the rest of the evening fixing his bike.'

'More than once he was the victim of our merciless campaigns,' added Lex. 'Once there was a lot of noise coming from one of the floors. Adri didn't like it one bit, but didn't dare sort it out himself. He never got much beyond "stop it, lads", so he rang the officer of the watch, Eddy here, to help him out.'

He clapped Eddy on the shoulder.

'Shortly after, the guy in question ran into the flat with his pistol drawn and shouted to Adri that he "would sort it out". On the third floor he fired his pistol, which was filled with blanks, at one of the cadets, who had slapped ketchup all over his shirt. Adri came running round the corner, sized up the situation and rushed off to call an ambulance. We managed to intercept him just in time. We chatted him up all evening to make sure he didn't report anything the following morning, but of course he did anyway. So the next evening it was the same story. A commotion in the lift, crammed full of guys with nothing on, yelling, "Adri, we're going to rape you, olé olé, olé, olé, we're going to rape you, olé olé, olé, olé..." Adri locked himself in his glass porter's lodge, nicknamed the aquarium, and when the naked cadets started pounding on his windows, he drew his service pistol. The din died down and Eddy offered his apologies on behalf of the whole group. But things were never the same again between us and Adri.'

'I spent eight days in a cell behind the guardhouse,' said Eddy dryly.

Niki, who had stood and watched the men in amazement, said, 'And now you lot have come to sort things out here?'

'If you don't mind, that is,' said Lex. 'Tonight I'm heading into the mountains with this gang, on a short patrol. I'm really looking forward to that,' Tijmen chimed in enthusiastically. Eddy threw an imaginary hand grenade.

'That's really too much,' screamed Niki, making a bee-line for the commandant, and leaving the men roaring with laughter.

Later in the evening there was an outburst between Eddy and Lex. Eddy was watching television which was showing non-stop porn films, but he saw Lex pointing to the girl behind the bar, a local beauty with long wavy hair who was scarcely sixteen.

'Lovely arse, firm and long,' shouted Lex.

Eddy slapped him in the face. Tijmen tried to calm him down, but Eddy stomped off angrily to their quarters.

'Plaits!' Lex called after him. All the venom of the last few days was compressed in that exclamation.

That evening the beautiful Lucia, the daughter of Alojz Mezga, was crossing with a UN soldier the three hundred metres that separated the camp from her home. Because the corporal who escorted her each evening had a fat face and a crew cut, she secretly dubbed him 'the pig'. When she was working behind the bar he followed her every movement with his beady eyes, but he had never bothered her.

At the road barrier the soldiers of the village whistled at Lucia. The 'pig' laughed and winked at the soldiers.

Lucia was a girl who, when she reached the age of fifteen, had suddenly turned into a beautiful young woman. Her breasts began to grow and for the first time she became aware of men noticing her. None of the village boys had the courage to ask her out, since her mother guarded her like a precious treasure.

She no longer had a father. 'Alojz Mezga died like a hero,' people said. It was during the first few days of the war, when the Muslims had launched assaults on the village, that the blacksmith had taken command of all the able-bodied men. The Muslims had been repulsed, but Alojz Mezga had been killed in the process, in the hills behind his home. Jakob, the son of Lačić Jaruja, had brought her mother a red handkerchief and a grenade fragment that had been found at the scene. These were given a place of honour on the chimney-piece, next to the wedding photo. Her mother had cried all night and the muffled sobs had penetrated Lucia's room. She herself had not been able to cry.

That same night her uncles and cousins had taken revenge, and scores of people died. Only the mullah and a few prominent Muslims had survived the massacre. They were forced to remain in the enclave as hostages. Alojz Mezga's body was never found.

To begin with Lucia and her mother had been able to live on the supplies they had hoarded at the start of the war, but when autumn came, everything became dearer. Before long a kilo of sugar cost ten marks.

One morning the white vehicles of the Dutch had driven into the village. They had rented the brand-new hotel from Janko

Ivan, the richest man in the village, at a steep price. And the very next day the mayor had visited her mother to ask whether she, Lucia, could work for the Dutch. 'In recompense for your family's sacrifice,' he had said. But the money that Lucia earned was paid directly by the Dutch to the mayor, who in exchange arranged for a food parcel to be delivered to her mother every Saturday.

After dark the music began playing in the headquarters of the Hollandski bataljon that rang through the village high street late into the night. People's tongues wagged but no one dared point the finger at Lucia, since the mayor was a powerful man.

The bar of the hotel grew busier each evening and Lucia started dressing more and more provocatively. Tight sweaters and black leggings that showed off her figure and went well with her long, reddish brown hair, which came down to her buttocks. Her young breasts went on growing and every day the soldiers' looks seemed to become greedier. She loved it.

This evening she had secretly observed the new group of soldiers. They were different: more arrogant, more professional than the soldiers she had seen up to now. Almost all were officers, who always stuck to the furthest corners of the bar. When one of them pointed to her, another had hit him.

That night the beautiful Lucia dreamt that they were fighting for her hand.

After the colonel left it went quiet for a moment. Then 'I'm gonna, rock 'n' roll with my little sex doll...' blared out of the speakers.

Tack-a-tack-a-tack ... The music mingled with a sound like pebbles being gently thrown at the windows.

Again: tack-a-tack-a-tack.

The bar emptied and Tijmen went outside too. There he heard the sound again, much louder now: machine-gun fire, in the hills behind the headquarters. In a long line along the hillside the fighters' campfires flickered. Now and then came the flash of a tracer. Each explosion was greeted with cheering by the spectators, as if the Dutch football team had just scored a goal.

It was like New Year. He was the well-paid spectator at the show, but of course he missed the highlights, because the fighting was mainly at night. The truckers here stayed anxiously in their camps, like the rest of the UN troops. The night showed its true face only when respectable people were asleep, in Soho in London, on the Reeperbahn in Hamburg and certainly here in this godforsaken country. But during the day they stayed in the valleys, as the Krauts had done fifty years before.

That night there was a sudden din outside the tent close by, the vicious blows of a hammer, voices yelling, running footsteps and a dull blow followed by a long-drawn-out cry. When Lex tried to open the wooden tent door in the morning it had been nailed shut. He forced it open with a well-aimed karate kick. Later Tijmen heard that one of the corporals had broken his arm in a nocturnal fight.

In the days that followed little happened. Lex and Eddy had settled their quarrel. There was as yet no prospect of a mission for Dutchbat, and the transport battalion gradually got used to their guests.

The officers played Trivial Pursuit ad nauseam, with Eddy losing time after time. Meanwhile Lex had started working out fanatically and in the mornings ran round the camp in his helmet and flak jacket, to the great hilarity of the truckers. One afternoon he was given a haircut by a sergeant, and was soon surrounded by a large crowd of onlookers. He had asked for an 'airmobile cut' and the audience that had assembled yelled enthusiastic encouragements to the sergeant.

Lieutenant-Colonel Verbeek had withdrawn to his room at the top of the hotel and, like the other colonel on the same floor, scarcely showed his face. The helicopter people, the quartermasters and the doc were a separate group anyway, to which Tijmen paid little attention in those days.

Although as a full colonel the deputy brigade commander – 'El Coronel' as Lex called him – outranked Lieutenant-Colonel Verbeek, the 'CO', Commanding Officer, of the battalion was the real commander of the reconnaissance party. When Tijmen thought of Verbeek later he always pictured him as bigger than he actually was. He had boundless admiration for Verbeek, further reinforced by the blind trust the battalion commander placed in *him*. It was as if Verbeek knew that was how he operated best. It was to be quite some time before Tijmen discovered cracks in his memory of Verbeek.

Verbeek, CO of the Grenadier Guards, Eleventh Airmobile Battalion – popularly known as 'the red berets' – was a rare combination of keen intelligence and front-line officer. There were smart officers, who were going to go a long way, and front-line officers. In external appearance Verbeek was a thick-set, jovial Brabanter, a huge figure with calloused hands and a bellowing laugh, a fat cigar clenched in his teeth, exactly as you imagined a commander, totally involved with the fate of his battalion. He was reckoned to be among the best in his year. Yet for some mysterious reason Verbeek had never been awarded the 'golden sun', the almost sacred insignia of Staff College officers. And it was only in exceptional cases that such a person was given command of a battalion, let alone the First Airmobile.

Despite his bad knees, Verbeek had successfully completed the strenuous final exercise to gain his red beret. He and his company commanders were among the first for a long time to start exercising 'on foot' again, the vanguard who had been on the very first death-defying descent from the climbing tower at the commando base in Roosendaal. He was also the one who in the spring of 1992 had asked them if they wanted to become red berets, and if they were willing to be sent 'anywhere in the world'. That was the moment when Tijmen had resolved not to die a virgin.

One afternoon, when the reconnaissance party had almost given up hope, Verbeek came in, red in the face. He was waving a fax.

'We've got a mission!' he cried.

The general staff in their underground bunkers in The Hague had finally spoken the magic word. The lieutenant-colonel was breathing heavily.

'The bulk of the battalion is going to Srebrenica, where there's a Canadian company at present, and you, Tijmen, will be going to Žepa with Alpha company. There are Ukrainians in Žepa right now. And Support Command,' he said to the quartermasters, 'will probably be located around Tuzla.'

He indicated the various locations on the map with a pointer. The engineers immediately started making calculations and the personnel officer left to arrange things with the Canadians and Ukrainians.

At supper all conversations were about the new mission. There was an unspoken rivalry between the company commanders, and before they left the table Lex had christened Tijmen 'King of Žepa'. From then on he used it himself, as a kind of honorary title.

The CO formulated his words carefully. In the weak wintry light coming through the skylight Tijmen could scarcely make out Verbeek's face.

'There's no need to write down any of this,' he said to Tijmen, who was sitting listening with his notepad on his lap.

The pungent smell of burning charcoal penetrated the room. Verbeek turned on his chair. 'There's a rumour that the Ukrainian commander was murdered. Perhaps by his own people. Of course there's an official version: that he trod on a mine. There are also stories about lively trading with both sides, deals with local whores, who are driven from post to post, and even the Ukrainian's weapons seem to be trained on the enclave.'

Tijmen looked at him in surprise.

Verbeek lit up a cigar and cleared his throat, 'I'd prefer to keep the battalion together, but I've been overruled. I just wanted to tell you...' He waited for a moment. 'You must tell me what you think you'll need, King.'

He brought the conversation to an abrupt close. 'Come on, let's go for a beer.'

That evening Tijmen told Verbeek that he thought Brokkel, the brigade commander, was a prick. He was frightened he was speaking out of turn, since he knew Verbeek and Brokkel had been in the same year. He described the shooting exercises in Bergen-Hohne, during which Brokkel – who was still only battalion commander – had belittled Tijmen, then second-in-command of the staff company, in front of his men 'because there was soap residue underneath the water truck'. Tijmen had never forgotten that humiliation. And in the same year Brokkel had ordered him 'to bring a young lady to the officers' mess parties at long last'.

'And the worst thing of all,' said Tijmen, 'was that he always refused to talk to NCOs and privates.'

The lieutenant-colonel rocked uncomfortably to and fro on his bar stool. A little later he was called away for a call from Holland. When he returned to the bar, shaking his head, there came the admission, muffled by coughing and smoke, 'You're right, King.'

He didn't want to say what the phone call was about, but Tijmen suspected it must be Brokkel's refusal to take a stand about keeping the battalion together.

The following morning the reconnaissance party travelled to Kiseljak.

The hotel housing UNPROFOR's Bosnian headquarters was bursting at the seams. Every day new wooden extensions were going up and every day the situation was becoming more chaotic. At the foot of the hill the vehicle park was slowly turning into an ever larger quagmire. Almost all the occupants of the hotel were officers from scores of countries, who left their workplace only when there was no other option. The hotel balconies were crammed with dish aerials, giving the building the appearance of a monster to which all UN units throughout Bosnia were attached by mysterious threads.

Lex and Tijmen had been instructed by the lieutenant-colonel to make contact with Section 5, which was responsible for liaison between military and civil authorities.

It was lunchtime and the dining room was full of officers in sharply creased trousers having lunch with their interpreters. Tijmen observed the interpreters: pretty girls in floral dresses. They had definitely not been selected for their proficiency in English.

Lex and Tijmen had just passed the restaurant when they were stopped by a Dutch lieutenant-colonel coming the other way. If he had not introduced himself as Lieutenant-Colonel Wijnands, they would have had no idea he was a senior officer. He would have been just a lean guy in a tracksuit.

The lieutenant-colonel wiped the sweat from his face with a towel. He was pleasantly surprised to meet two Dutch 'frontline officers'. He told the pair that only the previous day he had met General Cerković in person; the general had talked with great relish of 'Turks' he had killed with his bare hands. The Serbian had found it a great joke, while the UN officers had observed an embarrassed silence. Still, there was an undertone of respect in the lieutenant-colonel's voice. He said, 'Do you two know Cerković?' And without waiting for an answer, 'I *know* Cerković.' After a cordial farewell, Wijnands pointed them to Section 5, tucked away in a corner of the huge hotel and manned by a solitary Spanish major and a British corporal.

Tijmen briefly outlined the reason for their visit. When the major replied in broken English, Lex burst out laughing.

'Vamos a la playa,' he whispered in Tijmen's ear.

'Srebrenica?' said the Spaniard.

He rummaged in his papers and then looked despairingly at the corporal. Then went over to a computer and angrily pounded the keyboard. The screen remained black. He swore in long sentences. Lex translated, 'I shit on the twenty-four balls of the twelve apostles. I shit on the Virgin Mary, who is a whore.'

The corporal, who up to this point had looked on in silence, now also sprang into action.

Meanwhile Lex said to the major 'We also need maps.'

'What do you need maps for?'

'What do we need maps for?' echoed Lex.

'In case we get lost,' said Tijmen.

The major looked at them uncomprehendingly.

'Forget it,' said Lex.

'No, I have no maps, but you've come to the right place for information on the enclaves.'

Not long after Lex and Tijmen were back in the corridor. On the slip of paper it said: 'Srebrenica: approx. 40,000 inhabitants'. The voice of the Spanish major blared down the corridor, as he launched into a lengthy, but totally incomprehensible litany directed at the corporal.

Lex and Tijmen set out to find 'Holland House'.

Holland House was a rather grand title for the room they found. It was ruled over by a surly sergeant with thick rolls of fat at the back of his neck. There was a coffee maker, a refrigerator and a ventilator, while the walls were covered with the inevitable windmills and cows, and Dutch flags, which the members of the Dutch reconnaissance party had had to cut off their uniforms because they were too similar to the Serb tricolour. The officers present ignored the two of them. On the table were a couple of five-week-old Dutch tabloids, AD and *Telegraaf*. Tijmen was annoyed that he couldn't find any of the quality newspapers. In the past he would have just shrugged his shoulders, but the past seemed a long way away.

While Lex got coffee, Tijmen twiddled the piece of paper from Section 5 in his fingers. Just a few months ago, the third Tuesday in September, he had been at the head of his company at the State Opening of Parliament. True to tradition, Alpha King's Company of the Grenadier Guards, in bearskins, was marching ahead of the Golden State Coach. Forty-five minutes from the stables to parliament, a rest outside parliament during the Queen's speech and another forty-five minutes back to the stables of Noordeinde Palace. He at the head with sabre drawn; in front of him the Colour Party and the battalion commander with his adjutant, who were also listening for his commands. Fortunately he had a good commanding voice, which meant he could easily reach the rearmost ranks despite the din along the route.

For the first few years when he had taken part as a lieutenant he had been proud, but on that last occasion he had found himself constantly thinking of the tin soldiers he used to have. Nevertheless, he had been gratified by the compliment he received afterwards from the 'Governor of the Royal Residence'. He knew it meant nothing, but they were *his* men, Alpha King's Company, the first professional company in the army and the first red berets as well. It had been announced on the speakers along the broad, tree-lined avenue leading back to the palace and there had been loud applause from the stands at the news that the company was soon to be sent to Bosnia.

And *this* was the only scrap of paper he was given. Nothing about Žepa, where Alpha Company was expected to go and sort out the mess. Rear-echelon motherfuckers, goddamn logistics pigs. He made one resolution: should the company actually been sent out, he, Tijmen would personally make sure that everyone came back.

Verbeek himself now appeared in Holland House, waving with suppressed fury the half A4 sheet detailing the battalion's mission. He had been palmed off with it by an uninterested

British lieutenant-colonel. Cornimont, the commander-in-chief, was away on more pressing business.

As they walked back to the cars, Verbeek's officers found it hard to keep up with him.

Two days later the reconnaissance party was given an extensive briefing on Srebrenica at the Canadian battalion's headquarters in Visoko. For some reason the information had never found its way to headquarters in Kiseljak.

'We run our own show,' said the Canadian commander. That is what they were told at all the units they visited.

Tijmen left the room halfway through the briefing.

The sound was crackly and came through with time. A loud buzz came out of the earpiece, followed by Frank's voice, 'Ladies and gentlemen, could I have your attention, please. I've just heard that Captain Klein Gildekamp is on the line from Bosnia.'

Applause.

'Welcome, Captain, Major Platvoet here.'

Tijmen chuckled under his breath. Frank was laying on the formality again.

Frank's question was lost in loud crackling.

'Frank?'

For his first few years with the battalion he hadn't dared call Frank by his first name. Only when Tijmen was promoted to captain and they worked at the same desk did Frank say it was time to use first names. In those days Tijmen still felt slightly sorry for the major, whose greatest ambition was to surpass his father, who had made it to colonel. Something that was unlikely ever to happen, despite the efforts of Frank's wife, Veerle, who at parties invariably asked the CO 'when it would be Frank's turn'. And when she went on at him Frank simply withdrew to his room to fiddle with his beetle collection. Consequently Veerle would tell everyone willing to listen that 'Frank spent most of his time at home working in his study'. Lex did a good impersonation of his nasal voice, 'Veerle, this is nine zero echo,' the call sign of the deputy battalion commander, 'can we try it with me on top for a change?'

The sound was now clear. Frank repeated his question, 'Can you tell us where you are at present?'

'I'm with the Canadians in Visoko, where Lieutenant-Colonel Verbeek is currently being briefed on the situation in Srebrenica.'

'Can you say anything at this point about Alpha Company's mission?'

Tijmen was prepared for that question.

'Yes, well, almost the whole battalion is going to Srebrenica but King's Company is going to Žepa, or at least that's the intention.'

Of course at that moment someone in the hall in Orange Barracks was pointing out Žepa on the map.

'What do you mean by that?'

'That at the moment we can't get through. The Serbs won't let us cross to the enclaves, but we hope they'll give us the go-ahead in the next few days.'

'There are a few additional questions from the floor.'

A short silence.

A nervous father asked, 'How risky is the situation, Captain?'

'Oh, it's peaceful in the enclaves. Actually the biggest danger here is the traffic.'

Tijmen quickly added that spring was just around the corner and conditions on the roads would quickly improve. He said nothing about the tricky situation of the Ukrainians in Žepa.

Frank again addressed himself to the audience. There were no further questions, but a little later he heard his mother's voice down the phone.

'Hi, Tim here.'

The audience roared with laughter.

'Did you get our letter?'

'Yes Mum, and thanks for the cigars too.'

Then his father came on the line. They kept interrupting each other awkwardly.

Frank ended the conversation.

'Good luck, Captain, and we hope you'll be back before Christmas.'

Tijmen replaced the receiver. The Canadians in the communications centre were agog. Sweat was pouring from his forehead.

After the visit to the Canadians the convoy headed for Sarajevo. On the road signs the Latin alphabet had been replaced by Cyrillic script. A little later the convoy was stopped by a guard at a Serbian road block. The restaurant was decked out with Serbian flags. It looked almost festive.

Tijmen's attention was caught by a short, skinny man in a grey suit with a red padded jacket over it, looking around timidly. He had grey-blond hair, deep hollows at the temples, nervous twitching around his mouth and a small pointed nose. He was just like a mouse.

'Tijmen hesitated for a moment, and then stuck his head out of the window.

'Frits! Over here, Frits, over here!'

The man looked up and saw the Dutch convoy. His face broke into a smile and he rushed over to the lead vehicle.

'What are you lot doing here?'

'I could ask you the same thing,' said Tijmen.

Frits said he was working for the UN in Sarajevo. How long was it since he had last seen Frits, the historian, who had once served with the battalion as a conscript reserve officer? He had difficulty picturing the same fellow, six years earlier, as a young man.

It was on manoeuvres in Sennelager that late one evening he had drunk a bottle of whisky with Frits. The two of them had stood on the table and belted out songs, before finally falling asleep in a semi-drunken stupor. In the middle of the night he had heard a splashing sound. When he called out to Frits there was no reaction: Frits was peeing imperturbably over his locker. At his second shout Frits got the fright of his life, threw the door open and ran out into the corridor. Frits had vanished for the rest of the night, and the next morning reported back on duty red-faced with embarrassment. He had got lost and found his way into a building full of senior British officers, though he only realised the following morning.

'Where's Henry?'

'He lost his ID this morning and had to stay behind in Busovača.'

Frits chuckled.

There wasn't much time to reminisce. Frits was in a hurry, and went off to say hello to the lieutenant-colonel. Then he disappeared as quickly as he came. Into thin air.

A sweet red-haired girl in a purple ski suit, who was obviously in charge of the road block, raised two fingers and a thumb, standing for the Father, Son and Holy Ghost: the Serbian greeting. She casually made the sign that had become synonymous with death and destruction. Her breasts swelled under the tight-fitting suit. Lex made the sound of a zip fastener followed by the squeaking sound of a chamois leather cloth, as he rubbed his hand over Tijmen's bald head. A shadow fell across Tijmen's face. At moments like this he hated Lex.

The girl asked for their IDs, made a careful note of their names on a list and then they had to open up their vehicle. The blue helmets gave a nickname to all the local commanders. For example, the 'King of the Bridge' and the 'Prince of the Road'. That day the team thought up a new one: 'Chick of the Road'.

The convoy hurtled down the road. Manus the personnel officer, led the way, together with a guide from the Ukrainians, who had been assigned to the convoy after the road block. The road past the airfield was lined with steel sheets to protect the traffic from snipers. Music from the *Killing Fields* was blaring through the car from the tiny speakers of Tijmen's Discman. There was little oncoming traffic. The people in this part of Sarajevo were anxiously lying low.

In the centre there were only a few cars still driving about, none of them entirely unscathed, and all around the Eastern

European-style blocks of flats the car parks had been reduced to car cemeteries, as if an invisible giant had been playing heavy-handedly with the vehicles. Children were playing their own toy war among the wrecks with home-made wooden rifles. Their excited yelling echoed among the concrete colossi. Caught up in their children's fantasy they forgot the real war raging all around them.

Tijmen scratched his head. Only when they too no longer wanted to play at war would the conflict really be over.

Among the flats hung a thick pall of burning bonfires, the smell of sorrel soup and stewed cabbage. The trees had long since vanished: everyone had been hoarding for the harsh winter. In the hills you could see the exact course of the front line; it was where the fringe of woods had been hacked down. There was scarcely any electricity, and the supply was irregular. The balconies were full of neatly cut and sawn wood, and the ground floors of the flats were barricaded with thick, upright tree trunks: an effective protection against incoming grenades. Water was available only at central and dangerous points in town. For the past few days there had been rumours that the Serbs were trying to poison the inhabitants via the drinking water.

The dangerous stretches of the route were indicated in red on the map, and the Ukrainian covered them at top speed. In fact, Tijmen didn't know what was worse: the Ukrainian's driving or the ubiquitous snipers, who were turning the town into a kind of shooting gallery. He pulled the anti-shrapnel blanket attached to the inside of the door a little higher and braced. The constant rumble of artillery fire accompanied the vehicles. Sometimes there were signs with arrows on them at the roadside and beneath it the word 'snajper', as if it were a tourist attraction. The people in the street paid scarcely any attention. The women lugged jerry cans of water or fuel and bundles of kindling wood non-stop through the town.

Ambulances with sirens wailing regularly raced across town, taking new victims to hospital. On the pavement no one gave them a second glance. The steel girders of the ice stadium, which had been shot to pieces, where Katarina Witt had scored her triumphs at the 1984 Winter Olympics, protruded accusingly from behind the boundary fence. Figure skating was a great love of Tijmen's, as was ballet.

The medallions were still there in the pencil case. On one there was a depiction of the Virgin and Christ, on the other St Christopher. Double-pinned.

Tijmen could smell his socks through his combat boots, and his clenched fists were sticky with sweat. Yet what most attracted him were the women of Sarajevo, as if he wanted to ward off his fear by looking at them. They were not wearing headscarves and baggy trousers like those in the countryside. The people here were modern, as in every big city in the world. Precocious girls laughed at the cars with their bad teeth, wrecked by Turkish coffee and sickly-sweet, sticky baklavas, which were still available everywhere in Bosnia.

What was it that English journalist had written? It was about orphans. About a girl, Natasha. About the director of the orphanage, who said, 'Eventually she'll be like all the others. They're all the same. The boys will become thieves, the girls, prostitutes, and that's certain from their first day here.'

Halfway down 'Sniper's Alley' the convoy stopped at the 'Central Post Office Building', where part of UN headquarters was located. The lieutenant-colonel went inside with the colonel and the rest stayed in their vehicles. The car park was directly in the line of fire. Tijmen could hear the bullets whistling past. Further away, from the direction of the city centre, there was the sound of explosions, and small white plumes of smoke rose above the rooftops. Just like on the simulator at infantry school back home....

Old Pista Rácz took hold of the basket of loaves and dragged it into the dark shop. His son Béla smiled in welcome. He took the flat loaves out of the basket and laid them one by one on the shelves. He couldn't get them up there fast enough: the queue outside the shop was getting ever longer. Pista went out the back again and fetched more new loaves. After the fourth basket he sat down for a moment and lit a cigarette.

The customers stood silently in line, with red-cheeks and glasses misted up, enveloped in their thick coats. He knew most of them and when he gave a friendly nod, people nodded back. He was well regarded. He, Pista Rácz the baker, supplied bread. Only the doctors had higher status. They and Pista kept the silent faces alive. The people said: 'When the Jews leave, the town will be finished.'

Indeed, the vast majority of the Jewish community had already left, but Pista had stayed. His family had come to Sarajevo at the end of the nineteenth century, with the Hungarian occupying forces, and had never left.

His family in the Diaspora, spread throughout the whole of Europe and North America, had written long letters in an attempt to persuade him to emigrate with his family. Uncle David in New York promised to send money for the journey, and Cousin Saul in Lyon had offered to find him a job. All Pista had done was to write back polite but determined letters, and since Passover he had found a refuge for his wife Agi and daughter Agnes with friends in the countryside. They had not visited him since the summer. The old town was becoming more dangerous every day. But as long as Rabbi Steiner stayed, Pista would stay, and he knew that the Rabbi would never leave the town.

The queue outside seemed endless. Soon he would have to disappoint people again. Business seemed to be thriving, but people could no longer pay. So Pista accepted everything: goat's cheese, rakija, cigarettes and even clothes. His customers were now mainly Muslims. The greeting 'salaam aleikum' rang through the shop with increasing frequency. The other groups had left, and with them the range of bread on offer also shrank.

The matzos, which with approval of the rabbi he baked for exactly eighteen minutes, and the bread that met the requirements of the Koran. But also black Russian bread, croissants, baguettes, English pies and Viennese bread. He had been famous for his Schwarzwälder Kirsch, but now virtually all he baked were flat Turkish loaves. He was supplied with flour by the battalion from the Ukraine and occasionally from UNHCR. Sugar, though, was becoming an increasing problem.

At the end of the morning, when the last loaves had been sold, Béla pushed the people back. Pista had just put three padlocks on the door and was watching the unlucky ones slinking off with a dazed expression on their faces, when he heard the low growling sound. The glass in the windows trembled and father and son dived under the counter. The blast shattered the glass.

'That was a close one, Dad,' shouted Béla.

The old man looked round his bakery for the last time. A few seconds later there was a gaping hole where once Pista Rácz's shop had proudly stood, smouldering in the cold winter air.

The men in the car park were ignorant of events in the town centre. Arend, one of the sergeant-majors, came over to the group excitedly and grabbed Tijmen by the arm.

'Fuck!' he cried, 'Didn't you realise that those dead-heads had opened fire on us?'

'Listen Arend, if they get you, we'll just sell you for a lampshade,' said Lex.

Arend, one of the 'hardcore' NCOs, was covered from top to toe in tattoos. Under one of the images was the royal motto 'Je Maintiendrai', but something had gone wrong in the process and he had added the missing 'I' himself in Indian ink while roaring drunk.

Arend's language was as basic as Arend himself. Every third word was 'fuck' or 'shit' and whenever he had to go to the loo, he'd say, 'Just going to knit a brown sweater,' or 'Just going to pull a splinter out of my back.' He had an arsenal of swear words in five languages, could burp to order and regularly disposed of gobs of green slime that he had coughed up by spitting them a distance of at least three metres. He was also the only member of the reconnaissance party able to pee right over the Mercedes Benz jeep. Not even Lex could do that. Arend was the kind of person who, by the time you had known him an hour, had told you his whole life story, showing you the photos of the car wrecks from which he had been cut at various times, which he carried with him in his passport, as travel souvenirs.

The battalion commander was not gone long and they continued on their way. Just before the town centre the convoy turned left towards Tito Barracks, where the battalion from Ukraine was based. From one moment to the next the streets had become deserted and the houses ruins. Mangy dogs snuffled about the household waste that lay scattered in the street. Not a soul ventured outside: this was where no-man's-land began. Whole streets had been devastated and houses with twisted steel sticking out of them set on fire.

The barrier across the entrance to the complex was guarded fraternally by the Bosnian government army, the Armija Bosne i Hercegovine, and the Ukrainians. They shared the barracks, the same barracks that had broken the nerve of a group of Dutch NCOs: the liaison group had fled the constant shelling. Back in the Netherlands they had been court-martialled, and in the press were depicted as cowards who had left the Ukrainians in the lurch.

The stairwell of the barracks was full of the acid smell of dried urine. The whole building was in an advanced state of dilapidation, as were the drab Eastern-bloc uniforms of its occupants.

When everyone had arrived, the commandant gave a long speech in a small room; this was translated by the only English-speaking Ukrainian officer. Suddenly the audience were alarmed by a loud impact, and immediately hit the deck. As they brushed the chalk dust out of their hair, the laughing commandant tried to reassure them. 'Mortars can't hurt us,' hitting the wall with the flat of his hand.

During the briefing Lieutenant-Colonel Verbeek said he was worried about the evacuation of the wounded from Žepa. For weeks helicopters had been denied permission to fly over Serb territory. The Serbs sometimes made an exception for life-threatening injuries, but only a week before it had taken twenty-four hours to transport a badly-wounded soldier to Sarajevo. He hadn't made it.

On the way back to Busovača, where they were to await permission to travel to the enclaves, the convoy came to an abrupt halt just beyond Kiseljak. The lead vehicle skidded across the road at an angle. A Dutch jeep was blocking the way. They were at the border of the Croat pocket, which they had to cross in order to reach the transport battalion in the following Croat enclave. Now Tijmen also saw the road-block at which the car was stopped. A soldier at the barrier handed a Dutch major a small package and immediately afterwards the vehicle shot off at high speed.

Now it was their turn. Through a haze of rakija the soldier hissed that he would only let them through if they gave him cigarettes. The soldier was no different from any other soldiers Tijmen had seen en route: no insignia of rank, the same uniform, the same dreamy face. Only the red-and-white checked flag on his arm indicated what he was dreaming of.

'Smoking is bad for your health,' yelled Lex.

Tijmen quickly stubbed out his cigar. On the mountainside to the right, machine-guns gleamed in the December sunlight. If they were to open fire, their party would not have a ghost of a chance with their pistols. The Croat laughed and showed his teeth.

Eddy, in the passenger seat, tried to take a photo from behind his map of the rusty anti-tank mines next to the road block. He had forgotten that his camera had an automatic flash. The smile disappeared from the Croat's face, but the guard decided to let them through. There was some confusion due to the fact that Eddy had got out of the car to compliment the soldier at length on their 'splendidly constructed road block'. It was some minutes before Eddy was, with some difficulty, able to extricate himself from the situation.

When they got back to the transport battalion's compound, Henry was waiting at the gate, his face contorted into a grin. Just after the vehicles had left that morning he had found his ID.

'How was it in Sarajevo?' he asked with a sour face.

'Lovely babes, Henry, you really missed something,' laughed Lex.

The military policeman on duty reacted laconically to the suspicious goings-on with the package at the road block, but promised to institute a full investigation.

His sleeping bag still had a musty smell from old field-training exercises. Tijmen listened to the breathing of the sleeping men in the tent and to the restless sleep of the doctor, who had been ill in bed all week. The doctor's wheezing got on his nerves. From far away came the sound of shots. He tried to think of home. He wondered if they were still up. Home, where Bosnia had seemed a world away. Half-asleep, he counted the hours.

Suddenly he remembered the name of the British journalist he had thought of that afternoon. Michael Nicholson that was it, that was his name.

Tijmen tossed restlessly to and fro in his sleeping bag. He dreamed of a town where children play war games with ebony toys. Their fathers, foaming at the mouth, are dead, their mothers chop wood, too tired to die. In the churches faltering faith in progress slumbers, but in the ruined ice stadium applause is nailed to the girders. In the suburbs tanks lie on their backs like tortoises.

He woke with a start and heard Lex looking for the bed next to his. He kept quiet. He dozed off again to the flickering rhythm of the generator.

They were the faces of people at the roadside, dream stockades of nameless girls. Their high heels caught in gaps in the pavement. Sometimes they accept money in alarm and embrace the man passing by, with their dimmed bird's eyes, with a sudden glance that strikes home, with peroxide hair flaming like straw. They eat their bread of charity. A rose of barbed wire twists in their womb when the Miss election jury asks, 'Are you still a virgin?' They say, 'The prettiest girls have disappeared.' And the general sends them to the love front. In the alleyways of senses his words crack like bullets. The town that killed its brides eats greedily from their bellies at night.

The light shone through the windows of the tent onto the sleeping men. Eddy went on calmly snoring. To his right Lex was muttering incomprehensible words. The stove was roaring at its highest setting. Tijmen got up and tumbled drowsily into the winter night. There was enough paraffin in the jerry can to last them until morning.

Back on his field bed he rolled up and zipped up the sleeping bag over his head, like a larva in its cocoon.

The next few days passed in the drudgery of games and jokes. Every day requests were sent to the Serbs for permission to cross to the enclaves. And every day there were fresh refusals. Cees, the major in charge of operations, had already become 'Champion de Pétanque' three times and everyone knew the Trivial Pursuit answers off by heart. If doc wasn't playing, even Eddy had a chance of winning.

The colonel made furious efforts to persuade the crisis staff in The Hague to arrange another mission for the battalion. It was now two weeks since they had left Holland, and eventually the hospitality of the transport battalion would run out, but they didn't seem to be making much headway. Despite the colonel's desperate attempts, the chiefs-of-staff were not interested in a mobile role for the battalion in Central Bosnia.

The colonel felt a bond with these men. He had volunteered for the reconnaissance party in order to give the matter more weight. The brigade commander had reluctantly given his permission. Dutchbat had to make its mark. The new airmobile brigade had been under fire for months. They had the most resources, the best people, and what's more they were regulars. So there were whisperings in the army, 'They're like bloody marines.' Or worse still they were called 'airheads'. Everyone was waiting for them to fall flat on their faces. But since the men of the 'eleventh' had made him welcome and Lex had dubbed him 'Il Coronel', the colonel's regard for them had continued to rise.

After days of waiting for Serb permission, the lieutenant-colonel decided to leave for Tuzla in an attempt to reach the enclaves from there via the northern border crossing.

They parked their vehicles at the Tuzla Hotel in the centre of town. Eddy greeted a man in a white suit as if they were old friends.

'Ha, the winter painter,' roared Lex.

While Eddy described his experiences, Tijmen set out with Lex to check out the situation. When he got back he saw that Henry was trying to teach Dutch words to a little girl with blond curls.

'Plllease sir, bombon. Plllease,' she said.

Henry couldn't resist and gave her a handful of sweets. Immediately children popped up on all sides. At the hotel entrance they were stopped by a fearsome-looking soldier. Some hard blows were struck, and the children dashed away. The blond girl ran crying into the street, the sweets still clutched in her fists, like bounty.

Her curls stuck to her head. Her cheeks went purple. Faster, still faster she must run. She avoided the big puddles, and jumped over the smaller ones, looking round to see if the other children were following her. Her white socks were stained brown by the splashing water.

Jasmina ran home without stopping. She was one of those children left to their own devices. Her mother was far too busy with the youngest ones, especially little Hasan, only six months old. Dear little Hasan, who always smiles when you prod his cheek with a finger, who roars with laughter when you tickle his tummy. Who when you ask him, 'Say Daddy', just makes little burbling noises. I bet he's going to look just like Daddy.

She didn't know where her father was, and whenever she asked her mother she always heard the mysterious word 'Vareš': that dreadful word which shouldn't really be spoken. 'Vareš, Vareš, Vareš,' she sang teasingly, when her mother was around.

But mostly she roamed the streets. At first with her dog Boris, with curly black hair that made it almost impossible to see his eyes. Boris, to whom she could talk. Most dogs don't talk, but Boris was different. He knew the names of people in the neighbourhood, he knew whom it was best not to talk to, and with whom it was OK to talk. 'That guy in the kiosk is a bit crazy,' said Boris, 'and not nearly as nice as Esma at the baker's.' She always gave them a bag of crumbly biscuits. Boris was her protector. He also knew that Daddy would come back one day. Boris was a wise dog.

They knew exactly where the pickings were best, she and Boris. Around the Tuzla Hotel, where the camera crews were and the people in the white suits, the 'ice-cream men'.

One day her mother had said that Boris had to go. 'It's best if we take him to the vet ourselves, before he just disappears,' she had said. And besides, it meant 'one less mouth to feed'. Jasmina had put on her prettiest dress when they took him away, to a man in town. He had told her and Mummy that Boris wouldn't feel anything. But she was sure Boris had called out to her from the other side of the door. The tall, thin man in the white coat had come out and offered her a sweet. She had knocked it out of his hand. 'That wasn't very nice,' said Mummy. She had cried for a long time when Boris disappeared, and she hadn't spoken to Mummy for at least a week. Mummy was horrid. Daddy would never have done a thing like that.

'After the war,' said Mummy, 'we'll buy you a new dog.' But Jasmina didn't *want* a new dog. She never wanted another dog. Other dogs don't talk. She had tried it a few times in the street, stamping her feet with rage, and she was almost bitten by the neighbours' schnauzer.

From then on Jasmina had gone by herself to look at the 'white snake'. That was what she called the convoys with their flapping blue flags. At home she tried to write it for herself, in capital letters: W-H-I-T-E S-N-A-K-E. But she couldn't write very well yet and the school had been closed for as long as she could remember. Just as well, as Granny's house was on the way to school. Granny, with her post-deaf ears, who every morning stared tight-lipped out of the window trying to catch sight of her son. And whenever she saw Jasmina, beckoned her inside. She is the only one whose name Granny remembers. Granny doesn't even know that little Hasan has been born. And she is given orange squash in a soup bowl. And each time Granny asks if the 'soup' is good. She lisps breathless songs and runs her hands through Jasmina's young hair and her hands smell funny and she starts to cry.

But Jasmina isn't frightened, she is seven and also has a Barbie doll she can tell everything. Dear little Barbie doll with soft hair, which she now presses to her glowing cheeks.

The Tuzla Hotel was right next to the headquarters of the second Bosnian army corps. A week before a Serb rocket had landed nearby. The power station on the edge of town had been hit during the rocket attack. Since then it had been operating at half power and was a desolate sight with its smashed windows. More and more frequently Serbian arbitrariness alternated with the more focused shelling of strategic targets.

Puffing and sweating the men arrived on the ninth floor. Their flak jackets were tight around their shoulders. Tijmen shared a room with Eddy. The members of the reconnaissance party walked excitedly down the corridor. At last a real hotel again. Tijmen was seized by a holiday feeling, which vanished the moment he saw the cockroaches crawling out of the bathtub. On a side table there was information about the hotel. Eddy rang the number of the nightclub.

'No electricity, nema nista,' said the Bosnian guard downstairs in the lobby.

The next morning they were given an extensive briefing at the headquarters of the Scandinavian battalion, close to Tuzla. Every unit had its own smell. It was Sunday and it smelled good here, of coffee, cigarettes and fresh pastries.

'The whole mission is one big transport problem,' said the logistics officer. 'Our tanks took six months to get here from Belgrade and a large part of the material is still in Serbia.'

During the coffee break a young, shaven-headed Swedish captain told them about the report he had written on the economic importance of the war. In civilian life he was a policeman in Stockholm, but in the evenings he studied economics. He told them about the orphans of Tuzla, who were sold to childless couples in South Africa for three thousand marks. He said, 'Those children are the lucky ones.'

The officer continued with a story about mysterious transactions on the front line between the two sides, about tracks in the snow the next day and the goods delivered to Srebrenica by the UN that not long after turned up on the black market in Tuzla. They had been transported back right through Serbian territory, and the bags of flour marked 'SREBRENICA' found buyers at exorbitant prices. Sometimes the Serbs sold their grenades at a thousand marks a piece to other parties and near Vareš they had even mounted an artillery barrage against a Muslim village for Croat gold.

The members of the reconnaissance party stayed only one night in the hotel, since the Scandinavian battalion offered them a place to sleep at the field hospital not far away. 'But it's closer to the power station for Christ's sake,' Lex said.

When they talked about the episode later, the conversation always came round to 'Brünnhilde' – the fat Norwegian woman 'who could tuck her nipples into her belt' – who had responded enthusiastically to the advances made by Lex. And they never talked about the quartermasters – Lex now called them 'support commandos' – who had reconnoitred their new location on the industrial estate of Lukavac. When the support commandos got back they were covered in coal dust. The samples they had taken at the site would be sent back to Holland for investigation.

Once they tried to get across to Srebrenica at Alpha I, the border crossing to Bosnian Serbia near Kalesija, east of Tuzla, but in the car park at Rainci Gornji a UN observer had said there was no point. Tijmen didn't know then that he would later make his camp close to this car park.

To the east was the River Drina, from which at the beginning of the war the citizens of Srebrenica had fished the bodies of hundreds of murdered Muslims. Further north were the mysterious concentration camps of Bijeljina, and southwards, close to the Serbian border, Višegrad. This was the area where the different population groups overlapped like different geological strata. It was the land of the popes, the mullahs and rabbis, the Christians, the Muslims, the Jews and the gypsies. The land of the long hot summers and the long severe winters, of rakija, walnuts and prunes and the land of the centuries-old struggle between Turks, Hungarians, Austrians and Germans. For the first time in history the various ethnic groups were inexorably and completely separated along religious lines, old neighbours had become enemies and the country was saturated with rhetoric that tended towards murder. The hatred was hibernating around blazing hearths.

This war was more violent than any previous conflicts. And still the papers wrote that things had always been the same in the Balkans, that it was a 'powder keg'.

Vlado Durić opened the piece of paper and took out the sandwiches. He studied them from all sides and sniffed the goat's cheese. Then he wolfed them down, took a few stiff gulps from his hip flask and with his sleeve wiped the crumbs from the corners of his mouth. The rakija was burning his throat.

He loved these winter days, when your breath froze. To the extent that he could still enjoy things, since a moonlit night in the summer had changed his life. On that day he, Vlado, the easygoing woodcutter from near Zvornik, had turned into a brute. After a long day's work in the woods he had returned home. Normally his children would be waiting for him and he called out endearments from a distance. But this time there had been no reply. There had been no trace of little Petar, who always walked the last stretch with him and wanted to carry his axe. The door was open and he went cautiously inside.

Ever since, the images had been etched on his retina. He had always thought that the war would pass him by, in his house deep in the mountains above Zvornik; the mountain landscape where he had been born and bred, the woods where he had played as a child, the square in the village where he had met his first love. He had not completed school in town; he had become a woodcutter, like his father and grandfather before him. Only in the mountains did he feel truly happy. He had never been farther afield than Višegrad. He had once gone to look at the bridge with his children and every evening since then had felt he had to tell them the legend of the old stone bridge just before they went to sleep.

He had always been content with the little things: the excited sound of his children playing in the stream, and Sundays, when his wife wore her black silk dress. Biljana, who had sworn to him that the war would never reach their house. The stories had gone from mouth to mouth, and had penetrated even the smallest hamlet. Of course the rumours had reached their remote home too. He didn't understand much about religious laws, just enough to know that every drop of his blood was mixed. In his family Serbs, Muslims and Croats were united. He, Vlado

Durić, had always thought that he had no need to worry. This wasn't the first war to have passed the area by.

Vlado could remember the tiniest details: the scar on Petar's knee, from when he had fallen into the barbed wire, and the smell of toffees that surrounded the girls when they came home from the cinema in town with Biljana. It was only their voices – try as he might, he had forgotten their voices.

Vlado's nostrils flared wide and he threw back his head. He smelled fried bacon. Somebody further on was grilling. He thought of the Sunday afternoons they used to have at home, when his wife covered the table with the damask tablecloth and put out dishes of sweet pastries, pieces of cheese, and freshly baked bread from the oven. And the slivovitz they drank with it, while the children had lemonade. It was a world tucked away deep in his memory. The peaceful valley of his dreams no longer existed.

Furiously he took the whetstone in his left hand and the knife in his right. Three times to the left, three times to the right, over and over again, until the hand grasping the hilt ached. He held the blade up to the light and inspected the sharp edge.

Some men talked about what they would do after the war. But he had nothing to go back to. Usually he even forwent the day off they were given once every two weeks. In the beginning he had gone along with them to the village ten kilometres behind the front line. But he felt lonely among the men with their wild drunken antics, the fury that they took out on the houses of the 'Turks', and he shivered at the music that had recently become very popular: folk music backed with a pounding techno beat. He had walked alone through the streets of the village, kicking pebbles and deep in thought.

Up here in the mountains was where he, Vlado Durić, belonged. How long is it I've been up in the mountains? He wondered. 'It must be almost a year,' he muttered, feeling his teeth with his forefinger.

Further on, old Ratko was singing a song:

'Pick up your rifle
and don't let them keep you down
that's how the saying goes...'

Vlado grinned. Ratko thought singing was good for your lungs. The sergeant interrupted his thoughts, 'Durić, there's a gap in the barbed wire at the foot of the mountain. I want you to go with me tonight and close it.'

He nodded and stared thoughtfully after the NCO.

Nights on the mountain were dangerous, when patrols of 'Turks' combed the countryside. The thin line they formed was becoming weaker and weaker. Just last week two men had deserted from the platoon. They were fed up with war. Rumours were circulating that in spring there would be a large-scale offensive against Tuzla. But they'd been saying that for so long. Only at the beginning of the war had Serb troops reached the outskirts of Tuzla. But during the day they were still in command. They fired their mortars at will, every day at a different village. And very occasionally the 'Turks' fired back. Then they took cover in the big trench at the back of the slope.

Vlado peered in a north-westerly direction. At the foot of the mountain, where no-man's-land began and where the barbed wire had been holed, there wasn't a house left standing. Further away a thin plume of smoke spiralled from a chimney. There were still people living there, right between the lines.

He spat in the fire and took out his binoculars. It was cold on the mountain. From here you could see as far as Živinice, thirteen kilometres away. That was where the 'Turks' lived, whom he now hated. He followed the road past Dubrave towards Rainci Gornji, where the 'Turks' had a base, and Kalesija, the front-line.

Over there, north of the road, were the hills where the 'Turkish' infantry had its positions. The cowards didn't dare show themselves in the open, because if they did, he, Vlado Durić would call up artillery support and destroy them like rats.

West of Rainci Gornji a convoy of UN vehicles was crawling through the snow like a white snake. He grabbed the radio and yelled through his report. On the other side of Viz Mountain, out of sight of the Muslims, the men ran for their mortars. Wheels were turned and grenades put out in readiness.

The waiting began. An hour went by, but there was no movement. A little later Vlado saw the vehicles leaving and heading west.

That afternoon Rainci Gornji came under heavy fire.

The reconnaissance party, disappointed, had returned to Tuzla, where the message finally arrived giving them clearance to leave for Split.

The convoy made its way south-westwards, past Živinice, Stupari, Kladanj and the one-way quagmire between Olovo and Vareš, that had only recently fallen into Muslim hands. On the way they passed a village that people must have just left. All the houses were immaculately kept, but the doors of the houses and the church were wide open, in a shattering silence.

Finally the vehicles reached the wide E 761 motorway between Visoko and Vitez along the River Bosna, where they picked up speed. Occasionally they had to brake for wheelbarrows and wooden carts piled high with household effects, pulled by skinny horses or donkeys; for farmers with a few sheep and women with bunches of twigs on their backs. And sometimes the convoy was overtaken by a spanking new Mercedes belonging to someone who was obviously growing rich from the war.

After that journey there was another night with the transport battalion; the pizza song had lost none of its popularity.

The following morning the convoy took a wrong turn on the way to Vitez. It was Tijmen's fault as map-reader. They passed a bridge across a fast-flowing river, and in the main street of the next village Lex suddenly hit the brakes. There was a rusting mine chain across the road. Later Tijmen heard that fifteen hundred Muslims were camped in the middle of the village, surrounded by hostile Croats: 'Pandora's Box'. He hadn't even noticed.

Before Gornji Vakuf the convoy was again escorted by two British armoured vehicles, which swept the contours of the hills with their on-board weapons. In the middle of the village the battalion commander flashed the lead vehicle. They stopped to ask what the trouble was.

The village was under almost constant mortar fire. If you listened carefully you could hear the distant thud of fired rounds. For the whole of their reconnaissance mission Tijmen had felt that the shelling only began when they had passed, as if the population were being punished for their presence.

The CO got out ashen-faced and showed them the note he had received from The Hague by satellite link: 'Permission for departure deferred.' When a little later he checked the message in the British camp, it turned out that the deputy brigade commander, the support commandos, the doc and the helicopter crew were being allowed home. The battalion reconnaissance party under the command of Verbeek had orders to return to Busovača and await further instructions.

The deputy brigade commander took out a snow-white handkerchief and blew his nose at length. As the colonel's vehicle drove off it started to snow.

Spirits were at a low ebb and the men shrouded in grim silence. Eddy and Lex no longer even talked about what they would do to their wives when they got back.

For a further week the reconnaissance party made desperate attempts to cross the line of confrontation with the Bosnian Serbs, until the situation was resolved by a message allowing them to return to the Netherlands via Split.

The last evening in the lobby of the hotel in Split, surrounded by an abundance of glass and chrome with harsh neon lighting, was about as cosy as an Italian ice-cream parlour. The tables were constantly replenished with green bottles of Heineken Export. Alcohol and the frustration of the last two weeks, in which it had proved impossible to reach the enclaves, produced an explosion of singing and bawling.

Lex swapped his blue beret for a red beret that he produced from his pocket, and with his high-pitched, piercing voice struck up, 'Yogi is a master bear.'

'Master, master,' sang the men.

'Yogi is a master bear.'

One by one the members of the reconnaissance party joined in. Eddy low and off-key, Tijmen at the top of his voice, Henry, Manus, Cees and the NCOs as a background choir.

'Master, masterbate, mastur, masturbate, master, master...'
'Second verse... Cornimont,' called Lex.
'Corni's feeling rather horny, Corni, Corni... Corni's feeling rather horny, Cornimont.'

Although the UN commander-in-chief was the butt of the song, even the lieutenant-colonel had no qualms about joining in the following refrain.

'Corni, Cornimont...'

The swelling voices thundered through the bare lobby. There followed rugger songs, rousing refrains; military academy songs and marching tunes.

Lex screamed at the CO, 'Your year song.'

The rest fell silent for a moment, but the lieutenant-colonel climbed onto the table and gave a spirited rendition of his year's song. He still knew all the words.

When at the end of the evening they got up to go to their rooms, the British officer who had been sitting listening at the bar all the while, called out that he had enjoyed it.

'The English don't go in for masturbation,' said Lex.

The next morning, head pounding, Tijmen read a Dutch newspaper at Split airport.

> The reconnaissance mission is unable to reach the enclaves of Srebrenica and Žepa because of the obstruction of the Serbs. They have, though, had discussions with UN soldiers from Canada and the Ukraine based in the enclaves. A spokesman for the Ministry of Defence speaks of a 'setback'. The staff of the UN peace-keeping force in Bosnia will now consider the situation, according to the Ministry. According to the spokesman the return of the mission does not mean that the dispatch of new troops to the former Yugoslavia will be delayed. 'We are still working on the assumption that they can leave in mid-January.'

The aircraft climbed and Tijmen saw the country fragmenting into small offshore islands, like a slowly fading memory.

It wasn't busy on the road. There were still twenty-two kilometres to go to Amsterdam. Tijmen had escaped as soon as possible from the reception at the Protestant Military Association, just outside the gates of the Orange Barracks in Schaarsbergen, where the deputy brigade commander had welcomed the reconnaissance party. There was no sign of Brigade Commander Brokkel. The brigade had gone on Christmas leave, but the families of all in the reconnaissance party had been present, except for Tijmen's parents. He didn't like these kinds of events and would visit them later.

'What are you doing this evening?' Lex had asked.

'Going to see a girlfriend in Amsterdam,' he had answered with a wink.

In the city centre he parked his car on the Herengracht canal. He walked determinedly towards the alleyways between Singel and Spuistraat.

It was quiet. The light from the windows transformed the narrow street into a ghostly red umbrella. Three times he walked past the same blond girl, who was looking wearily out of the window. Deep-set black eyes. He went in.

'I need to take a leak,' said Tijmen.

'That'll be twenty-five extra,' said the girl in broken English.

She was wearing shiny red boots. On the wall hung several leather outfits and a whip.

'I mean I just need to take a leak.'

Again the girl said, 'That'll be twenty-five extra.'

He gave her three notes of twenty-five.

The hallway behind the room was full of rubbish bags. In front of the toilet was a wastepaper basket, full to the brim with condoms and wads of kitchen roll.

A little later he was back in the room. The girl had already taken off her boots. It was over quickly. He got dressed.

'I'm a soldier,' said Tijmen. He was alarmed at his confession.

'They're always soldiers,' sighed the girl, 'or builders, or lorry drivers. But sometimes they're artists or men with briefcases. They come in their lunch break.'

Again she sighed. He asked where she came from.

'Croatia,' said the girl shyly.

'Hvala, thanks,' said Tijmen.

At the door she caught his arm. She brushed his sports jacket, as if he had been to the barber's.

In the street dripping wet from the rain, a thought hit him with the force of a kettledrum. During the reconnaissance mission he had scarcely exchanged a word with the local population, not even with the beautiful Lucia.

Tomorrow was Christmas Day.

PART II
INTERBELLUM

Each station that brought him closer to Breda made Tijmen feel more acutely how he was denying his past. He was like a culprit revisiting the scene of the crime.

In a stifling bout of apathy, he had spent the first few days of the Christmas holidays in his flat in Arnhem. All he had done was go to the baker's every morning, buy a paper from his local kiosk, then wander around the park.

And now, in the middle of his Christmas leave, he was on the train to the Royal Military Academy in Breda, where his career had begun twelve years before and where he had first met David. They had always been inseparable, he and David: sitting in the senate together, travelling to infantry school in Harderwijk in David's Beetle together, joining the Grenadier Guards Regiment together, and gaining their red berets together. Only to David had he talked of his love of poetry, about the parties in the officers' mess that he hated and to which he went alone, as he used to go to the soirées at the Royal Military Academy. David didn't understand either, but David was David.

David, who worked as a captain at battalion headquarters, had not been with them on the reconnaissance party. Tijmen had missed him. He had not been able to share with anyone the seeds of doubt sown in him during the reconnaissance mission about the role he was playing. Perhaps it was the same uncertainty that took hold of him when he talked to his father about the Second World War.

'No, Gijs never wanted a decoration. He wouldn't talk about it. And yet he was head of the resistance. We just knew. Sometimes I delivered letters for him to...'

His father glanced at him and thought.

'Arnhem, Ommen, Sneek, Assen... But that was only at the end of the war, you understand.'

His eyes grew moist. He didn't even notice the fact that Tijmen's mother kept butting in. Hard of hearing on one side. Handsome face, with artistic, white hair. Bald on top, of course, just like Tijmen. On holidays in guesthouses this sometimes created quite a commotion: he was mistaken for the CEO of a large company.

'At the beginning you didn't notice much of the war. My friend Thomas, though, hung the garden gates of all the Dutch Nazis from the lampposts. To be on the safe side, he hung up our gate as well. Gijs was furious.'

He laughed and his belly shook.

'In the autumn of 1940 Gijs joined the resistance and at the beginning of 1941, as a cover, he became a crew man on a barge in Gendt. The brother of an insurance agent of father's had a shipping business there.'

Tijmen asked about the names of the group members, but his mother jumped in first.

'Vermeer, Vincent Geelhoed, Joop Salverda, the Van der Venne brothers, who were shot later...'

'That's right,' said his father. 'Robert, that was Vermeer's first name. They always met at Joop's place in Museum Kamstraat. That's where the transmitter was too, if you ask me.'

His father awkwardly picked up his cup. Since the mild stroke his hands no longer functioned properly. His body retained liquid. As a result his hands looked even bigger than they were. Hands that had once hoisted Tijmen up for piggy-back rides.

'The rest of the guys at home went into hiding, but then they were quite a bit older than me. One by one they went through the checkpoint with the suitcase put together by Feitsma. They simply got out again on the other side of the train and were looked after by the ladies Holland.'

'Yes,' said his mother, 'the ones who ran the clothing store in Van Welderenstraat.'

His father talked right through her. He became claustrophobic in shops. It was in a clothes store he had suffered that stroke.

'Only when the parachute landings started did the penny drop. The Americans had a uniform with them for Gijs, with the royal motto 'Je Maintiendrai' on it. And on the Tuesday after the landings Joop Salverda came to see Father. For the first time I was allowed to stay while they talked. Even Granny had to leave the room when someone from the resistance came by. "The bridge has been saved," said Joop. That was the day Joop was killed. That week I put on my scout uniform for the first time in four years.'

His eyes were glistening behind the thick glasses; there was a green deposit between the lens and the frame. Tijmen remembered his father's stories about the jamboree in Vogelenzang. How he had been entrusted with the prestigious job of lighting a camp-fire. It was raining. He had put petrol-soaked rags among the branches. The burst of flame had been seen by all. At this point his father always imitated the sound: 'Whoosh!' How the public had jeered – he wasn't bothered. Later he had given his scout hat away to a boy who lived nearby. To this day he regretted it.

'Why do you want to hear all this?'

'No special reason,' said Tijmen, 'just to know.'

'No,' sighed his father, 'Gijs would never accept a decoration.'

Wasn't fighting for your country the best thing in the world? But Tijmen wasn't a bruiser. He'd never yet hit anyone. Or been hit. The grating of steel on steel hurt his eardrums. 'Tilburg West', he read on the signs. The images from the past had such a hold on him that the voices in the compartment merged into a background hum.

The first weekend of his course at RMA, the Royal Military Academy, he had proudly worn his uniform. Everyone on the train had looked at him. Ha, ha, ha, Tijmen in his immaculate uniform. That first weekend off he had had an insatiable appetite. It was called 'base-camp hunger'. Excitedly he had shown his mother his combat suit, from which the dirt had only come out after it had soaked for a week.

The next stop was Gilze-Rijen. Somewhere in the distance lay Camp Prinsenbosch.

When they arrived at the camp they had been given just enough time to put their things in the tents. Tijmen had been surprised that David was billeted in the same tent. David, who had chosen the bed next to his.

A harsh voice blared through the camp, 'Fall in!'

They were drawn up in squads of four and presented to the officers and NCOs, who stood to attention one by one. Their platoon commander was the huge buffalo of a guy in the line who answered to the name of Jansen. The sleeves of his combat jacket were rolled up in such a way that his formidable biceps were visible to all.

A fine leader of men.

'Lieutenant, to you,' said Jansen after the captain had handed over the platoons, before going on to say that everything in the camp must be done at the double.

Tijmen carefully copied what David did. He was lost without David. David knew exactly how you fixed the webbing to your small backpack. 'We'll have to blanco it shortly too,' he said, showing Tijmen a tin containing a green substance.

Meanwhile David had been promoted to tent orderly and what's more to platoon orderly. No one was keen on that job because it made you stand out, but David didn't seem to mind at all. 'Better than "laundry master" at any rate,' he whispered, when he was appointed. Even when he was urged on by Jansen to chase stragglers out of the tents, he helped them out calmly. 'Everything in a measured way,' as David himself put it.

Two weeks' training followed. The very next morning they had to do the Cooper fitness test.

'Don't go flat out,' hissed David, just after they had started. 'In two weeks' time they make you repeat the test and you have to score higher.'

The train slowly gained speed. There was a low mist over the fields. Tijmen could still recall exactly David's conspiratorial tone. These were useful things that only David knew. Dodges for quickly climbing back up again if you rolled out of a rope. Heating up blanco to make it easier to spread over the webbing. How to break in the stiff combat boots under the shower, which prevented blisters. But also: never go flat out in physical effort, there was always more to come. Always be in the middle of the food queue. If you were at the front you were 'antisocial' and first in line for fatigues, and if you were at the back you got the squashed food from the bottom of the food container. 'And your laundry number,' David always said, 'is more important than your name.' Nothing could reduce your chance of success quicker than badly fitting socks or chafing underwear. And in the evening, if you had a quarter of an hour before lights out, put your things out ready for next morning; it saved time. Eventually he became very expert in copying David. David said things like 'good plan' and when someone dithered, 'Don't make a meal of it'. After a few days everyone had said those things: 'good plan' and 'don't make a meal of it'.

Tijmen could even recall at the drop of a hat the smell of the camp: a mixture of freshly mown grass and stuffy tent canvas in the boiling sun. One afternoon they had suddenly had an hour off. Most people lounged about on the sports field. He had quickly gone to his tent to read. A moment's escape from the commands, the arbitrariness, the endless days.

He could only read with no one else around. But also reading was being alone. He liked being alone. He liked thinking, thinking and reading. Even at primary school. In the lunch breaks: his mother walking as quietly as possible through the room so as not to disturb him, crispbakes spread with sprinkled chocolate and coffee with lots of milk and sugar, 'kid's coffee' as his mother called it. His sisters' books, Enid Blyton's *Pitty* series, or the *Havank* crime novels from his parents' bookcase, went in two afternoons. Books were synonymous with events and events with books. *Max Havelaar, Or the Coffee Auctions of the Dutch Trading Company* was forever linked with a sea-scouts' camp: *Max Havelaar* was both the heat of the Indies and high summer in Friesland. *The Lion of Flanders* was hundreds of pages in the first form of high school, impressing that gorgeous Dutch teacher and staying down a year. And Baudelaire, Baudelaire would always be associated with Prinsenbosch camp.

David came in. He took the book out of Tijmen's hands, studied the cover intently and then the places marked with white paper strips.

'Baudelaire, *Les fleurs du mal*...'

David clicked his tongue.

'Listen, Tijmen, I'm sure it's interesting, but I simply never read poetry.'

He laid a hand on Tijmen's shoulder.

'Be sure to go on reading,' he said sarcastically.

'But Tijmen,' said David, whispering now, 'I think it's best if you don't show the others.'

Then he left the tent and called back over his shoulder, 'Rules of the game,' as if he were apologising.

That evening David told him about his past as a commando, crazy stories about 'the final commando training exercise', about 'night jumps', about killing chickens ('the heart's like chewing gum'), about his father, who had also been a commando, and his brother who had done his national service with the marines. He also talked about 'survival runs' and the hut he had at home where he kept his climbing equipment. David was a fanatical mountaineer. He concluded with a 'good commando tip': 'Make sure you don't get wet, because if you get wet, you get cold. And if you get cold, you die.'

It was rather odd advice, it was boiling hot, but their tent mates were all ears. David had power. Tijmen wanted to be like David. David winked at him. No one saw.

It was quiet outside Breda railway station. Tijmen inhaled the cold winter air. He left the morning sounds of the station behind. His civilian clothes hung loosely on him. Different from his military uniform, which supported the body, confined it. In uniform everyone was equal.

He straightened his back, and with the firm gait of a professional officer joined the stream of people heading for the centre, a fixed smile on his face. Soon he would be back in Bosnia. He felt like shouting it out, 'Out of the way, arseholes, with your "the world mustn't let that happen".' No, they couldn't do it for themselves of course. They let him do their dirty work. Well, if they really wanted to know, he was happy to go. Rather than pine away in a barracks in Holland. 'Anyway, it's none of your damned business,' he hissed, fighting back his nausea.

He took the same route as long ago, when he had had to appear before the Army Officer Selection Board.

The committee sat in one of the rooms in the main building of the Royal Military Academy. There had been five others besides him. The guy who went in before him had a face covered in blackheads and was wearing a blue suit. The legs of his baggy trousers reached far over his shoes, though he was the only one apart from Tijmen wearing a tie. After three-quarters of an hour he came out red in the face, greeted by a roar of laughter.

'What happened?' asked the other candidates.

'The chairman asked if this was my own suit. I replied, "No, and this tie is my father's too",' said the guy beaming.

It was only later Tijmen learned that Paul, which was the guy's name, had a wardrobe consisting mainly of flowered shirts and lycra stretch pants.

Without realising, Tijmen had reached the park. The outlines of the Castle were visible among the trees. This was the park that the sergeant-major sports instructor, who was also a judo champion, walked around each evening. Tijmen remembered very well how during sports lessons he would always say, 'You never know if you can make a difference to other people.'

The big doors swung open. 'Mr Klein Gildekamp, we're ready for you now.'

There sat the committee. Eight men and one woman, all in uniform; with faces leathery from a lifetime braving the elements. Most must have long since reached retirement age. The committee secretary had impressed upon Tijmen before they went in, the importance of not shaking hands. He went immediately over to the small table intended for him in the middle of the room. Minutes went by, a clock ticked in one corner, papers were shuffled and the pen of the man who had been observing him for quite some time, scratched across the paper. The sweat poured non-stop from Tijmen's face. His back felt clammy, the tight collar of his shirt cut into his neck and his gluteal cleft was wet with sweat.

The silence was broken by an officer who asked, 'Klein Gildekamp, is that a double-barrelled name?'

'That's right,' said Tijmen, 'there are Groot Gildekamps too. But we belong to the poor branch.'

At the request of the committee he listed the names of all the foreign secretaries of the NATO member states, which he had learned by heart. They kept on questioning until he faltered. A whole procession of writers and painters passed by. He had a fifty-percent chance of a right answer. When they got to Chagall, he had to give up.

'A writer?' he hazarded.

'Doesn't matter, Klein Gildekamp. After all, we're not training intellectuals here.'

'Finally, Tijmen,' said the chairman, a retired general, 'why do you want to go to the Royal Military Academy?'

He'd practised this one.

'A sort of vocation, doing my bit for the country, challenge and physical action...'

The chairman, who was more like a nice granddad than a general, interrupted him.

'You'll hear from us within a week.'

He was accepted. For the infantry. He was going to become someone. Later he had always said it was because he had seen the resistance film *Soldier of Orange*.

Tijmen was halfway through Valkenberg Park. He stopped by a bench, sat down and turned his collar up high. Facing him, on the opposite bank of the canal, was the parade ground, deserted.

To think that it had all started there, on the parade ground, where he had learned to give drill commands. The platoon on one side, he on the other. The sergeant who showed him how to do it. 'Volume!' A commanding voice could span great distances. For a short while the new rules had beckoned seductively, as if they offered certainty. Somehow he had lost that certainty, and disengagement had set in, entangled in abnormal grotesque thoughts.

It was in the middle of the parade ground that he had first met David, waiting for transport to Prinsenbosch. That was just after his head had been measured, size 57. David had a muscular build and large protruding ears. Tijmen had estimated him at size 60. There were deep grooves in his face. A handsome, weathered face. Defiant was perhaps the best word. Something in David's attitude appealed to him. He showed no trace of the nerves that Tijmen had seen among the other guys. David was older and projected sovereign calm: a certain combined nonchalance and arrogance. At that moment Tijmen had decided to stick close to the green-beret.

The same day David had put an arm around him. He said, 'I'm going to protect you, little chap.' Tijmen could well believe he had looked at the time as if he could use some protection. But David also said, 'If you follow my advice, little chap, you'll make it.' David called him 'intelligent', but said it as if he were referring to an unpleasant illness.

Tijmen rubbed his hand over his bald head. Whenever anyone made a remark, he always said that he had quite a few male hormones, or, to ring the changes: 'an hypophysis the size of a potato'. That hadn't stopped them calling him 'Granddad'.

David was the first to call him that, because of the bald head, not because he was two years older than the rest. David was five years older. At that time five years was a real generation gap. David still called him Granddad. When others said it, he shivered. Beyond the parade ground was the castle, Henricus. Beneath the gate were displayed the names of his predecessors. Their names had been scratched on every stone. In some cases the year of passing out had been added. He could have inserted his own. Passed out 1986. But he hadn't.

Through the gate was the inner courtyard. He had stood on parade there every morning for three years. This courtyard was paved with cobbles and enclosed on three sides by long colonnades. Above the arches were terracotta medallions with the profile portraits of famous Greek and Roman figures. The courtyard was the focus of the whole history of the Royal Military Academy; you could hear mysterious voices whispering from a distant past.

He had been dragged into the first-floor Great Hall on his backside. That was a 'significant moment', which you would 'remember as long as you lived'. It was one of those things that linked RMA officers: 'I saw you come in on your arse.'

In the Great Hall there was a strict pecking order. The second-years were the most dangerous of all. It wasn't even malevolence; it was the natural privilege of seniority. There was an even higher grade you could attain to: the inviolability of the third-year student. They treated the bulls, as the first-years were known, with a kind of calm certainty. This glamorous future was held up to them: the status of senior-years. 'Gentlemen,' they had to say. At that time Tijmen had scarcely seen any fourth-years; they were deployed in army branch training centres up and down the country.

Someone gestured to Tijmen that he must report to the next chair. He heard himself speak.

'Permission to pay my respects, Sir.'

'Van Boven,' said the guy.

His own hand was wet and clammy; the senior-year student's felt cold.

'Bull Klein Gildekamp, Sir,' he said in a plummy voice.

Van Boven said, 'We're not that keen on posh sods here.'

The guy wiped his hand on his trousers and prodded Tijmen in the small of the back. His eyes were fixed on his crown. This was the meat inspection.

'You're going quite bald, bull.'

It was best if he didn't say that bald men had a hypophysis the size of a potato. He had to pretend, had to go through the motions.

'Sit, bull.'

He tucked his feet under his chair and took out his notebook. Van Boven, a guy with a bulbous nose and deep-set black eyes, twisted his thin lips into a cruel grin and said, 'No info, bull, you've got to get some beer, because you're sweating.'

Tijmen was about to get up, but Van Boven pushed him back.

'How many beers, bull, how many?'

He spat the words into Tijmen's face.

'One beer,' stammered Tijmen.

Van Boven knitted his bushy eyebrows into a frown.

'Two?' asked Tijmen tentatively.

'Well done, bull. Off you go!'

There was a warm draught in the hall, which welded the sounds together, though sometimes a loud voice closer to him stood out. He had to keep to the centre of the hall. To left and right his fellow first-years were being intercepted with the same mission by ranting gentlemen.

Always keep to your first assignment.

When he got back to the infantry box, Van Boven took both glasses, eagerly emptied one and tipped the contents of the other down the back of Tijmen's neck.

He had been bewildered at the beginning. David had enjoyed the initiation, but he, Tijmen, had been amazed at his own metamorphosis. The ease with which he adapted. His eagerness to belong. Actually more than that: he wanted to be the best. It had taken almost a year, and then he was among the best and was more popular than ever, a hundred-metre sprint champion. Nowadays he hated every form of physical exertion.

For years the initiation had been an event that had joined the rest, covered in a thick layer of dust. The way he had talked about his years with the regiment was the same way he had talked about the Academy, anchored in a web of stories he had woven around himself. Those memories had held his past together and preserved the illusion that his life was in his own hands.

Only much later had he started thinking differently about it. As he had changed his way of thinking about everything. When everyone said one thing, he would think the opposite, just to have the feeling that it mattered who he was; the compulsive ideas he dreamed up. Don't march in step, out of step. Bullshit. He had always been one of the boys.

During the initiation he had been taught songs: the anthem of Limburg, the Infantry song and the solemn 'Bon Jour', which was sung at the end of every party. He had forgotten the words to most of them, but he still knew the Cadets' Song off by heart.

> You brothers-in-arms, the Netherlands' sons,
> come, joined by the same life's aim.
> By the same sacred passion inspired,
> with love of one country aflame.
> Strike up, strike up the song,
> and bare, and bare all of your heads,
> and take with us the self-same vow,
> and take with us the self-same vow,
> that formerly our fathers took
> when foreign violence made them sigh,
> that formerly our fathers took
> when foreign violence made them sigh.

Perhaps it was the proud words of the Cadets' Song that first fuelled his feeling of malaise. Perhaps it was his own pride that he was ashamed of. Images of his last year at school came into his mind.

'Gildekamp!'

Brouwers was standing next to his desk at the back of the class. Tijmen sat in the last row in every subject.

'Klein Gildekamp,' said Tijmen, correcting him.

'So, are you going to answer?'

This was his moment of glory. He had waited for years for this. He was older than the others. Twice he'd stayed down a year. Eight years was enough. He looked for Heather, sweet girl's girl with her high-pitched laugh.

'I was thinking of the RMA.'

A few boys laughed. Ton, who sat in front of him, turned round and looked at him wide-eyed. Only a week before he had told Ton he was going to study law, or go to business school; or if necessary join an ocean-going ship, as long as it paid well. That was what everyone in the class wanted: to earn lots of money. He had said to Ton, 'I've got the feeling I can succeed in any field.' Heather's face betrayed no emotion at all. Hey there, Heather, over here! He'd just announced the most dramatic turning point in his life...

'Yes, Gildekamp, you seem cut out for that.' Brouwers turned to the class, 'Of course it doesn't matter a bit if you're not quite sure yet.'

He stopped at the front of the classroom.

'And what about you, Heather?'

'Medicine.'

'Well, that's a nice subject,' said Brouwers, 'an important contribution to the community.'

Heather laughed. Brouwers stared straight at Tijmen. After the lesson the teacher came up to him.

'Have a good think about it, Gildekamp. I've always really liked you, you're so bloody likeable.'

He nodded, hurried down the corridor and out of the school. He was going to be a general.

Tijmen was cold. Occasionally people passed. Apart from that it was deathly quiet in Valkenberg Park.

What was he supposed to say if someone recognised him here? 'Come on, I think to myself, I'll pop down to Breda?' Unlikely. It was vacation.

He took a tin case out of his pocket. He lit up a thin cigar, took a deep puff and blew smoke rings into the air. He had learned to smoke cigars as a third-year cadet, from Hugo Defrel. Hugo, who always said, 'A cigar must be treated with the same gentleness as a woman, and so must only be lit with cedar wood.' That was when he was in the Cadet Corps Senate. Funny, 'Senator' was also a cigar.

The senate wasn't military; it was part of student life. Everyone wanted to get into the senate. He was elected. Study results also played a part. He had never been a top cadet, he hadn't won a single governor's medal and he had not even passed out with a commendation. David had. He had passed 'with merit', even though his mother had called out 'oaf' at the top of her voice in the stands as the diplomas were presented, because he had failed to get a 'with distinction'. But he, Tijmen, had never had to repeat an exam. And by the third year he *was* someone.

Over there was the senate chamber, in one of the corner turrets of the castle, with a view of the sacred stones of the parade ground and the trees of Valkenberg Park beyond. An impressive room with imitation antique furniture and wood panelling; a long wooden table and on it a large silver statue and two copper candlesticks, and high-backed chairs, which were carried into the hall by junior-years for every corps meeting. Next to the table was a small mobile canon. There was also a large wooden cabinet with scores of volumes of the cadet almanac, and lots of copper and silver objects which were regularly polished by the first-years under the direction of Mr Defrel, *Chef du Protocole*. One wall was entirely taken up with a precious painting, the counterpart of which supposedly hung in the royal palace of Het Loo. It was perforated in many places by the darts of illustrious predecessors. On the large candelabra in the middle of the room lay two crossed sabres. It was through all these objects that the room really came into its own, and there was no more distinguished place in the whole Castle; this was the Holy of Holies. For a whole year that senate chamber had been his domain.

'I give my word as a cadet to be at all times honest, loyal to the corps, and obedient to the senate...'

Only once, in his time, had the authority of the senate been defied. Two fourth-years caused a great commotion by leaving the corps. He, like all the others, had deplored it.

Tijmen clenched his teeth so hard they ground. Once he had lived for big words and ideals; if the words 'duty, honour, country' applied to anyone, they applied to him. His own panic caught him by surprise, his glorious past lay spread out before him. Eleven years later, and still he had got nowhere.

When Tijmen left his flat the morning after his visit to Breda he felt as if he were being spied on, as if someone were looking silently down on him. He slammed the hall door behind him and passed the people who had assembled outside the door of the mental-health facility down the street. He walked the streets rather aimlessly, his jaw taut and a deep frown on his forehead. He left the car where it was. He was in need of a bit of air. It was cold. Again he felt as if someone were stalking him, but when he looked round there was nothing to be seen. At least, no more than usual, since it was the kind of neighbourhood in Arnhem where you could just toss your rubbish bags into the street from your balcony.

He continued his walk through Sint Marten. Actually he didn't live here, but a little further away in the Transvaal district, wedged between Sint Marten, the much chicer Burgemeester quarter, Sonsbeek Park and the embankment of the Arnhem-Zwolle railway line. Actually the Transvaal district had nothing going for it. Not the cosiness of the traditional working-class Catholic districts of Sint Marten and Klarendal, and not the distinguished houses with bay windows in the Burgemeester quarter and Hoogkamp, where the rich Protestants used to live. The only sight was the canal in De La Reijstraat, with the private house on the corner where from ten in the morning to ten in the evening the light welcomed visitors inside.

He stopped at the cash-point in Hommelseweg. After putting the money carefully into his trouser pocket, he was faced with a choice. Through Klarendal to the Spijker quarter? He could also just go and sit in the park. But then he would probably have to listen to that man on the bench; that chap with his two bright blue hyacinth parrots. 'The Rolls Royce of parrots, sir.'

He didn't know what was worse: going to ground for a week in your flat, or the crazies and tramps in the park who started saying hello. Should he go to a pub and spend the whole day listening to what people were saying? But he scarcely went to pubs anymore. He preferred drinking at home, alone.

Without brooding further he walked down the canal. The winter sun was low over the railway embankment. Bent forward, eyes focused on the pavement, he quickened his pace, leaving small white clouds behind him like a locomotive. This wasn't a street for hanging about in. He could still feel the invisible shadow on his back.

In the tunnel under Velperpoort station he let out a yell and listened to the way the echo moved along the tunnel. In Steenstraat he stopped now and then outside a shop window. He used the glass to survey the other side of the street. The shopping public walked on imperturbably, as if they all knew where they were going.

Tijmen liked the anonymity of the town. Here no one knew who he was. He was only home at weekends and for holidays, like now; more frequently he was on manoeuvres. He hadn't even met his neighbours; since he began working in the barracks he left the flat at six-thirty and didn't return until late in the evening.

Two children chased each other, laughing. Some passers-by looked round for a second, but no one paid any attention to him.

The Spijker district was deserted. Only in the Turkish coffee house was it busy and cosy. Men in grey sports jackets were sitting in a fug of blue cigarette smoke, some playing dice, others cards. From a distance you could see the red glow of the windows, even now, in the middle of the day. Three women were standing together on a corner, one winked.

He made a detour to avoid the kerb-crawling cars. Most windows were not yet occupied. It was still early and the houses were being energetically scrubbed. At some windows there were dark-skinned women, who tapped on the window with their rings. He looked straight ahead. A few women were dancing at the window to inaudible music, a silly spectacle. Now and then one of them smiled at him, like an actress in a soap. At the very end, on a corner of the street, sat a pair of blond women. They looked inquiringly in his direction with their hard eyes. Just as he was about to turn round he saw a gorgeous girl leaning vacantly against her glass door.

He went weak at the knees and got goose pimples all over his body. The girl was the only one who was wearing no lingerie, but instead tiger-skin tights with a white top. She had broad hips, a flat tummy and nice breasts, long brown hair and a soft face which even in full daylight had delicate features. Most striking of all were her eyes. Big eyes with the deep, dark, brown of a wood in autumn. Rather sad, too. Tijmen walked another circuit and when he passed her a second time the sadness vanished from her face.

The moment he crossed the road he had the feeling everyone was looking at him. But the men in the street, backs bowed, continued on their way past the windows, sometimes hesitantly before they went in, and hurriedly when the job was finished. His face flushed. He must make sure no one saw him.

Tijmen celebrated New Year's Eve at home with his parents. For the first time alone with his parents. His elder sister had not come over from London this year; his younger was expecting her second child, and their old neighbour, Van Nieten, had died. Van Nieten, whom the local kids had called 'the Grim Reaper with a hat on'. Who every New Year's Eve told them about his father's business. 'We had twelve coaches! There were no cars in those days. They only came later.' There was no point in asking Van Nieten many questions as he couldn't hear them anyway. After his monologue and three gins he went home with his wife Charlotte, who had sat next to him in silence the whole while. But not before he had said to Tijmen's father, 'Well, neighbour, that was very pleasant as usual. Until next year then.' One year Van Nieten had forgotten to finish his story. That was when Tijmen's sister had drunk champagne for the first time, and when Van Nieten came in she had kissed him on both cheeks.

Tijmen pressed the bell and smelled the familiar scent of 'oliebollen', Dutch doughnuts, which his father, as was his custom, had deep-fried that afternoon. Oliebollen, and traditional red meatloaf, were his father's domain. Tijmen said hello to his mother, who gave him a worried look.

'You're feeling OK, aren't you? You're eating enough, aren't you?'

'Yes, Mum, stop worrying.'

She must have seen something about him. Tijmen couldn't keep much from his parents. They supported him unconditionally, just as long ago they had supported him when he had said he wanted to go to the RMA.

'You're a special lad,' his mother had said at the time.

With every promotion they had been bursting with pride. They had always been proud of him. He remembered that performance at primary school, when, wearing his grandmother's dress, he had recited a poem about an old football boot. Only his parents had clapped.

In the kitchen his mother told him she had agreed with his father that they wouldn't get alarmed if a military vehicle suddenly appeared in the street. All through December his father had lit the big Easter candle in the living room. When his mother looked at him like that she was just like the Queen of England looking at her favourite horse before a big race. The same short, stocky figure, the pouting mouth, the worried eyes. He gave his mother a kiss on the cheek.

He told her about the painting he had done, a self-portrait in all shades of red. He had been painting for a few years, but up until then always abstract. His mother thought it was a 'macabre' idea, so soon before he was sent out.

When Tijmen returned to the living room with a dish of oliebollen and apple fritters, he saw that the Easter candle had shrunk a few centimetres. The same candle that had burned at all the important moments in his life.

'The Allies, my boy, if it hadn't been for them,' said Tijmen's father.

When his father, on holiday in London, had first stood face to face with Big Ben, his eyes had filled with tears. Radio Oranje, broadcasting from Britain, was the sound of freedom.

Behind his father's eyes lay the shadow of the war; that was his benchmark against which everything was measured. The world consisted of two kinds of people: those with whom you could go into hiding and those it was better to steer clear of, war or no war.

'When we came back to our home in the Betuwe after being evacuated,' said his mother, 'the piano was in a ditch next to the house. The British had used it as a footbridge. Not that we minded, because the British were our liberators.'

Only the collected works of Dickens had survived the war. For forty years the volumes had had place of honour in Granny's glass china cabinet, the leather bindings curling with the damp.

'Shh, the lad doesn't want to hear all that.'

Tijmen could have repeated their stories in his dreams, but he wanted to know everything. His parents were elderly. How old had they been then? Fifteen, seventeen perhaps. According to his father he, Tijmen, was born just after the war. That was seventeen years later.

'Uncle Gijs learned to shoot in the back garden. He was picked up by a car every morning. Uncle Gijs was part of the Military Authority. When the girls who had gone with the Germans had their hair shaved off in our street, he intervened personally. Later Uncle Gijs visited the camps on behalf of the Dutch government. After that he didn't go to Germany for a long time. He always drove in a wide arc around it.'

'So did we,' said Tijmen dryly.

They'd only been in Germany together once. It was in 1968. By this time his father had already swapped the van with the logo 'Zwanenberg no waste but great taste' for an Opel. 'Unfortunately a German vehicle,' his father always said, 'but from an American design.'

It was a drive of a little under three-quarters of an hour to Kleve. Even in the car park his father had got into an argument with a German directing traffic. 'Can't you just see him in a helmet?' he said. According to his father, Germans were born to wear helmets. They had gone straight back home.

'Dad, why weren't you in the forces yourself?'

'High blood pressure, unsuitable for sending to the Indies. I asked them to put it in writing. That medical officer was furious. Thought I was a coward. So I explained to him exactly why I had lost confidence in the government. How many people who had done their bit during the war, in irregular squads and suchlike, were given the cold shoulder? I would have gone more or less berserk in the Indies.'

The war had meant that his father had not finished secondary school. He had worked his own way up in business. Although his father didn't call it that. He said, 'Industry'. No one was as heroic as his father. No one.

While they watched TV together, Tijmen heard himself talking in a carefree way about the reconnaissance mission.

'Are the oliebollen OK?' asked his father, interrupting his flow.

'Pretty good, but I think they're even better cold.'

'I'll pack a few for you later, Tim.'

The TV was showing images of Bosnia. His father zapped to another channel.

At midnight they raised their glasses, 'Happy New Year'.

'It's a very special year,' said his mother, 'although it will be difficult to be without you again.'

His father growled something unintelligible and kissed him on both cheeks. Then the fireworks erupted. Tijmen stayed indoors. Whenever a squib went off, his reflex was to hit the floor. The same thing that had happened all through the Christmas holidays whenever a door was slammed shut in his block.

The first day after the Christmas holidays Tijmen drove early to the barracks in Schaarsbergen. He noted the friendly respect with which he was treated by the sentry; the parade ground with the monument to fallen grenadiers, the battalion flag waving in the wind alongside the Dutch tricolour, the determined strides with which soldiers hurried about the barracks, and the squirrels that darted away into the bushes.

He parked his car in front of the company building, got out and walked to the entrance. At the door he was startled by his own reflection with its hollow eyes. In the hall two soldiers were clearing away the Christmas tree. They glanced up as he passed. He strode resolutely to his office, greeting men from his company on all sides.

Speedy, his deputy, was already there. He told Tijmen about logistics, which were a mess, stumbling over his words and gesticulating wildly. 'Speedy' was the name Michel had given himself. If he had been an animal he would have been a racing thoroughbred.

'A cigar, Granddad?' asked Speedy.

'I'd prefer it if you'd stop calling me 'Granddad' and use my proper name.'

Tijmen lit up his cigar and looked reflectively at the smoke as it rose. He had over a quarter of an hour before parade.

He wondered if Speedy actually minded always being addressed by his nickname. A terrible name, 'Speedy'...

Eight o'clock. Morning parade. Tijmen grabbed his baton, wedged it under his left arm and hurried outside with Speedy at his heels. The baton he carried was decorated at one end with a hand-carved head of a grenadier in a bearskin, the same bearskin they wore at the State Opening of Parliament.

It was cold outside and Tijmen decided to keep it short. Herman, the company sergeant-major, had drawn the men up in ranks and reported.

'Com-pa-ny... stand at... ease.'

At the last clipped command a hundred and thirty pairs of boots landed with a single thud. The company would follow his orders to the letter. But apart from these formal commands they would do everything else he said as well. Sometimes he would go into town with a group of men, and he was quite sure that if anyone tried to lay their hands on him, his soldiers wouldn't hesitate for a moment. If he gave the right commands now the company would start moving around the building, beneath the lieutenant-colonel's office. Left, two, three, four... If it went as he wanted, only on each first step, 'Left'.

'Stand easy.'

The company sank a couple of centimetres and relaxed.

Tijmen told them briefly what had happened on the reconnaissance mission. The soldiers' eyes were burning with curiosity. The rumour that the December reconnaissance mission had ended largely in failure had raced on ahead of him.

After the company had fallen out his eyes glided along the rows of red-berets quickly seeking the warmth of the building. At the back were the men of the second platoon, half of whom had had a small red beret tattooed on their shoulders during Christmas holidays.

Remembering is thinking with your eyes open and shut. They were like the props in a play, images etched higgledy-piggledy on his memory. The first few weeks as recruits, when forty percent had dropped out; the stiff final exercise in the Eifel mountains and the steep rock wall near Nideggen; the presentation of the first red berets by the minister at Deelen airfield, for which the press had turned out in force; the white clay of the army training ground on Salisbury Plain in Southern England, where he had almost lost an eye during an airmobile attack and the karaoke evening in the pub where they heard the doc sing for the first, and after some insistence, last time; the skiing lessons on the Zugspitze in May bare-chested, when they all got sunburned; the shooting exercises in Bergen-Hohne...

He tried to remember the names of the army training grounds: Ginkel Heath, Lauwersoog, Sennelager with the 'Führer Tower'; Haltern with the inn just past the sign saying 'All units Wulfen', with the jukebox full of sentimental patriotic songs and men who banged their knuckles on the table in greeting, a local custom, though he didn't know that at the time... And the Four Days Marches in which he took part with the whole company. The flag parade in Goffert Stadium where he had marched past with his men, round the cinder track and right through the puddles that the marines in front of them had carefully avoided. They were airmobile troops and would not be stopped by anything or anyone. On the last day of the Four Days Marches he had promoted two NCOs to staff sergeant. In one go they had emptied their boots, which had been filled with beer, mixed with the sweat of four days' marching.

In the afternoon the company commanders were summoned to see Verbeek.
Tijmen was late. Eddy, Lex, Henry and Manus were already there. Verbeek paused for a moment before sitting down and beginning again.
'It may be a little while before we're actually sent out.'
From outside came the sound of commands. A platoon of red-berets surged towards the teaching building. The CO distributed the schedule with the order in which they were to leave. All that was missing were the dates. How happy Tijmen would be when things got started. He'd been waiting for this for years.
In the short silence that fell as the company commanders each looked for the schedule for their own company, Henry mentioned that he had turned forty. He produced a box from under his chair.
'Stari čovjek,' laughed Lex, maintaining that it meant 'old man' in Serbo-Croat.
Manus cut the cake with his pocket knife and served the pieces. For a moment the only sound was that of tinkling coffee cups and forks scraping over the plates.

'From my wife,' said Verbeek, and with some embarrassment handed Henry a package in red wrapping paper. It was four bottles of beer. Henry blushed.

Verbeek got up and started pacing about the room.

'As far as I'm concerned, the men can use up as much of their back leave as possible in the next few weeks. As long as someone is left behind that I can do business with.'

Verbeek stopped by his desk and lit up a cigar. The same desk at which Tijmen, received his bonus every year. One of twelve in the battalion every year; especially chosen for his commitment, for the overtime he put in. Ha, ha, there was nothing for him at home. He had never felt so alone.

'Let's have a quick look at the diary before we leave,' growled the CO.

They went through the activities for the weeks ahead. The cheap light-brown veneer on the walls, the chairs with the grenadier's grenade on the arms, which had been carved by Verbeek's father, and the dark-blue carpet with the same grenade in yellow, gave Tijmen the feeling that all this would stop one day. Just for a second, and then he dismissed the thought.

In the afternoon he visited David, who worked at battalion headquarters, but David was busy and had little time for him.

After supper in the officers' mess, Tijmen worked at his desk for a couple of hours. This was the nicest time, when calm had returned to the barracks and he could do his work undisturbed. Now and then he left his desk to walk round the men's quarters.

Again those expectant faces. And again he had to disappoint them. 'Probably Žepa.' 'No, there's no departure date yet.' 'Leave in Žepa? Highly unlikely.'

The disappointment was tangible.

Very late in the evening Tijmen returned to his flat in Arnhem, where the silence weighed on him. Eight years in the same flat, where time's mechanism had jammed. No one had been loved here.

He was closer to war than ever. There had always been wars, and there would always be wars, but this, this was his own war.

The tension he had always dreamed of. The memory of the reconnaissance mission lodged in his head as if a bell jar were being placed over him. He no longer even heard the train passing his window.

'There's a storm brewing,' say the soldiers by the roadside. In the distance a snow plough draws furrows through the land. I exchange some words and ask, 'Is this Yugoslav?' 'Never use that word,' says the toothless one and then casually, as the barrier falls, almost apologetically, 'There's no way back.' We founder of necessity on the British camp. 'Duvno' says the map, but the signs speak of Tomislav, a Croat warlord of the tenth century. At night there are white beans in tomato sauce with offal and from plastic cups lukewarm lemonade. In the north someone plunders the towns and villages at night, someone chalks slogans on a wall. The colonel greedily drinks in the breasts of the girl on page three. He leers. We lug our heavy bags to a chilly hall like lambs to the slaughter. No one ventures outside. Neon strips spew fountains of electric light to the flickering rhythm of a generator. The horse, the wall bars and the parallel bars with unequal cross-sections: the idle cold steel. The great leader – Tito himself – who stands silenced in bronze on his pedestal. The night shattered into dream splinters. Through lips of clotted glass rattles the 'bora', which – till spring with thunderous force cleaves winter asunder – blows its treacherous lullaby.

It would definitely not be long before he could call himself 'King of Žepa'. It was all chance, inexorable. His nickname of 'Granddad' exchanged for another.

A song came into his head. Thijs's voice. When Thijs was still artillery liaison officer with the battalion, he always led the singing during drinking sessions in the mess and on Friday night in the bivouacs:

'When this lousy war is over,
No more soldiering for me'

PART III
A SMELL OF WAR

It had taken yet another two months before the battalion was sent to Bosnia. But now, at the beginning of March 1994, troop movements were in full swing. Eddy had already arrived in Srebrenica with his Bravo Company. Lex was still in the Netherlands with Charlie Company and Tijmen's Alpha Company was in a hotel on the Croatian coast waiting for transport. During the reconnaissance mission in December the company commanders had been forced to throw in their lot together, but now they were physically separated, little was left of their 'triumvirate'. This had given way to rivalry, with each of them wanting to excel with his company.

Tijmen had been angry when he learned on his arrival at the hotel that Žepa was not going ahead and that the whole battalion was being sent to Srebrenica. But once he had realised that his anger was not directed at anybody in particular, he had resigned himself and had set off as soon as possible with David, ahead of the troops.

Tijmen was glad he was travelling with David. This time it was no coincidence that their paths were crossing. The lengths they had gone to in the hotel in Brela to get away! And the second day David managed to obtain permission for both of them. An end to uncertainty, far away from those dreadful boat trips out to sea, the cultural excursions to Dubrovnik and the tough mountain hikes to keep the men happy. He had got out of that nicely. Otherwise he would definitely have plodded along behind, as he was about as fit as a doormat. That was what he always said, 'Like a doormat.'

They had taken a helicopter for the stretch from Split to Tuzla and spent the night with Support Command in Lukavac. The first thing Tijmen heard as they drove into camp was the pizza song again. The old coke plant was being slowly converted into a military camp by the logistics people. A group of whores were gathered outside the gate as they were every evening; he had even seen how the guard regulated transactions. From a weathered portrait in the corridor of the main building Tito glared severely down at the intruders.

The former industrial estate was covered in coal dust that clung to boots and clothing. Every time the wind blew, the fine dust swirled under the doors. In the buildings there was a thin film of it, which worked its way into every nook and cranny. There were rumours circulating that it could make you ill.

There in Lukavac, Tijmen had heard that David and he were to be allowed to cross to the enclave of Srebrenica with a busload of journalists, right through Serbian territory, escorted by a convoy from the transport battalion.

In Lukavac, David had had only one pair of underpants which he had rinsed out in the evening. This morning they were not dry enough and David tied together the Aertex shirt he wore – it stopped you sweating, so he maintained – with the blue UN lanyard. And every time he looked at David now Tijmen couldn't help thinking of the insignia of the UN soldier being worn like a thong. He laughed to himself. You scarcely ever saw British or French combat troops with the lanyard, but you did see observers and the logistical units wearing it.

The fast-flowing mountain water of the wide Drina was greenish black, and turned as grey as the sky as sleet fell gently into the water. There was no one to be seen on this side of the white chalky bank, the silence hung like a hovering bird of prey over the woods. On the far side was Serbia. Although there were scarcely any people visible there either, that bank still made the more inhabited impression. You sometimes saw an onion-shaped church dome, and then some smoke from a chimney which mingled with the fog that shrouded the steep summits. In some places the pine forest was interrupted by farms and small villages.

On the far side of the river there was an asphalt road, but that was out of bounds for UN traffic. There were no cars on it – the boycott against the Serbs was paying off. Serbia, so close and yet so far. It might just as well be another world, with the Drina as the inexorable border.

It was an adventurous landscape, almost like in a fairy-tale, and yet as threatening as Tijmen had seen it previously. Between Tuzla and Zvornik it had been ominously deserted, more rugged too, with bare rocks and low undergrowth creeping towards the roads on all sides. That was the area 'cleansed' of Muslims, where the 'Prince of the Roads' held sway. Not until they reached Zvornik had he seen any kind of activity.

'What time do you think we'll get there, Captain?'

Tijmen turned round to the man who had spoken, one of the journalists at the back of the bus.

'An hour, I estimate,' said Tijmen, studying his fellow-passengers.

Two of them were young, the TV news reporters. The rest of the bus was filled with slovenly middle-aged men. At the front sat the major accompanying them, and right behind him David and himself. It was as if there was an invisible but tangible pecking order, with the reporters at the back at the top. Odd that in the flesh they always looked so different than on TV; much shorter than you would think, and with coarser faces.

It was stuffy in the minibus into which the men were tightly packed. Tijmen could feel the stiff cotton of his combat trousers sticking to his legs. He wished he were in the fresh air, with the cold fog in his face. He pressed his cheek against the window, leaving a greasy patch. The sky grew more and more overcast. No more sign of the hint of spring he had felt earlier. The minibus jolted at snail's pace over the bumps and potholes in the road. Sometimes the water splashed higher than the windows.

A small chap with a black fringe of beard looked malevolently in his direction. He was the only one not to have introduced himself on departure. Over his paper he asked almost solemnly, 'And what's your function, soldier?'

'I'm the ex-King of Žepa,' said Tijmen on impulse, 'or, to put it another way: the uncrowned ruler of Žepa and surroundings.'

David chuckled. Someone called out something from the back of the bus, but they couldn't hear it at the front.

'Shame it didn't come off. It would have made a bloody nice ski resort.'

Tijmen leapt out of his seat and with one knee on the floor and the other at a ninety-degree angle, made an impeccable Telemark landing.

The little guy interrupted the demonstration with a string of words that sounded like clipped expletives, 'What the hell are you doing here?'

'Trained to kill, my body is my weapon,' said Tijmen, filling his lungs with air.

'Idiot,' said the rasping voice.

Tijmen reacted with a gesture halfway between a shrug of the shoulders and turning his back in pique. He was on his guard, as he had been taught. Out of the corner of his eye he saw the little guy pursing his lips. A moment later the poison dwarf was again deeply absorbed in his paper.

But Tijmen changed his mind. He couldn't help himself, and apart from that it was as if the chuckling David was egging him on.

'And what do you do, friend?' he asked the man.

'I'm in charge of the greetings programme,' he hissed in annoyance.

'Buy a Beetle then!' cried David.

For some days he had been using that slogan at every opportunity. At the back of the bus several suppressed a laugh.

'Really, a greetings programme,' said Tijmen, his face breaking into a smile, 'so unless I'm wrong you make a living from our greetings home?'

Now it was the journalist's turn to shrug his shoulders.

'I wonder if there'll still be snow?' said David

'I don't think so,' said Tijmen.

'Do you know,' said David thoughtfully, 'actually you should count yourself lucky.'

His remark surprised Tijmen.

'Being sent out with a company, it must be a fantastic feeling.'

He sighed. Tijmen remembered his friend so well as a company commander, but since they had become red-berets, David was languishing at staff headquarters. How did he put it? 'Slaving at staff is no laugh.'

'Perhaps we'll be murdered,' said Tijmen gloomily and continued, 'It's best to be prepared for the worst, then you can only be pleasantly surprised.'

'Yes,' said David, 'then you can only be pleasantly surprised.'

The journalist on the other side of the aisle complained about the stale lunch packs in the voice of someone able to blow up trivial snags into insurmountable problems. Tijmen controlled himself. After all, they were guests of the battalion.

How many days had he been away now? Three, he calculated. It seemed much longer.

The bus came to an abrupt halt. In the distance there was a bridge and the last checkpoint before the road turned inland, towards Srebrenica and away from the Serbian river border. Someone gestured for them to get out. In silence they lined up. When the Serb reached the group of journalists he studied their ID at length. Then he shouted something to his commander.

Excited orders were given, and a little further on the convoy leader was involved in a fierce discussion with a group of Serbs. People were pointing in the direction of the bus. Soon after, the convoy leader disappeared to Bratunac to consult with the Bosnian Serb authorities.

Dusk was already falling. The Serbian commander of the roadblock got onto the bus. The man had a fat, fleshy face, and his paunch bulged over his belt, from which two hand grenades dangled casually.

The Serb gave the passengers a furious look. Someone unobtrusively took a photograph of the scene. He turned to the journalists and began a long monologue in a hotchpotch of English and Serbo-Croat words. He spoke so emphatically that gobs of spittle flew all around. Sometimes Tijmen caught a few German words mixed with the rest: 'Für Sie sind wir Serben Mörder!'

When the man had finished, Tijmen felt like applauding, but a glance at the hand grenades restrained him. With a curt gesture the Serbian policeman ordered the driver to follow his vehicle.

Lazar Zekić smoked one cigarette after another. There were nicotine stains on the fingers of his right hand. Cigarettes were the only luxury that Lazar, the straightforward policeman whom the village children called 'fatso', could afford. Since he had been in charge of the roadblock, he was ensured of an unending supply. The UN convoys were glad enough to be able to buy an easy ride with cigarettes.

Lazar turned to his driver.

'Those Nazis think they can pull the wool over my eyes,' he scoffed.

He had immediately recognised the face of the boyish man at the back of the bus. He was the reporter from the Dutch commercial news channel, which they could receive with their dish aerial at the town hall. There, an interpreter carefully monitored every report on the Dutch battalion.

'UN Aid Worker, who do they think we are!' he exclaimed.

The driver shrugged his shoulders. Lazar didn't see, because at that moment they passed the bus stop which formed the watershed in Lazar Zekić's little war. There was the period before the incident and the period after.

It was during the first months of the conflict when he heard shots outside, followed by a swelling, low-pitched weeping. A crowd had rushed to the bus stop jeering. They raised their clenched fists. Someone waved the Serbian cockerel. At the stop stood the Osmanagić family: Mehmed, his wife Olga, and their three children, two boys and a girl. Beside them were the belongings that they had brought with them in their great haste.

Lazar had been at school with Mehmed, long ago, when people still talked about that other war. In those days Lazar had come to school in short trousers, even on icy winter days. Not Mehmed. He wore long trousers well before the others. The brilliant Mehmed who always got good marks. A boy with a bright future beckoning. Mehmed was later to take over his father's business. He, Lazar, would probably end up on the assembly line at the factory, in the opinion of the teacher, but Lazar hadn't gone in that direction. He had become a policeman.

The crowd had come close to the bus stop. At that moment Mehmed gestured to his wife and children. The children had hurriedly crossed the road and made for Lazar's house. Olga had followed hesitantly, as if she didn't want to leave Mehmed behind, but Mehmed pushed her roughly towards the house.

Olga had remained icily calm, but the children were very upset when they came in. Lazar could still clearly remember their tear-stained faces. His wife had wanted to make coffee.

From his window Lazar had seen the crowd seize the belongings from under Mehmed's nose. Mehmed stood clutching the last suitcase. Blows were struck. A moment later the factory manager was on the ground.

Then Lazar did something he had never thought he would have the courage to do. He rushed outside, pushed back the attackers and helped Mehmed to safety in his house. The injuries weren't too bad. There was just a trickle of blood from Mehmed's right eyebrow.

People had flocked outside his house and chanted furious slogans. Only when a window was smashed had he put on his police cap and gone out to calm them down. They had listened to him in silence. The first to speak was Damir, the burly striker from the football club.

'Come on, behave like a good patriot, Lazar,' he said.

Lazar had not contradicted him. Damir was the new leader of the village. If anyone could protect them from the Muslim militia, it was Damir. At the time there were rumours circulating that their village was the next target of the Muslim fighters. Oh no, he didn't want any trouble, no trouble, please.

He had never seen the Osmanagić family again, and he had never asked about them. For the first time in twenty years he, Lazar Zekić, had been given a promotion. He became chief of the police post.

What could he do? It happened everywhere. With the 'Turks' and the 'Ustašas' too. After the incident he had carried out his duties even more diligently. It was nothing to do with him, Lazar Zekić.

Dusk had turned to deep darkness. Bratunac was the first place in Bosnia that seemed to show scarcely any traces of the war. Even the street lighting was on as normal.

In a flash the minibus passed the thickly painted white houses with their plastic flowers at the windows. A little further on sat a cigarette seller, the kind you saw everywhere in Bosnia. Sometimes they sat at a Formica table, while others, like this one, had a wooden tray with their merchandise on it which they carried on a long strap round their shoulders like market traders.

In front of the hotel where the vehicles pulled up people who had come flocking from all sides advanced menacingly. They spilled over the car park like a spring storm and leaned on each other's shoulders to get a better view of the spectacle: a single tugging and pushing mob.

'Look, it's the peacekeepers,' they jeered.

When everyone had assembled in the lobby of the hotel the people outside pressed their noses against the glass. In the ensuing chaos the journalists were informed that they would not be given permission to continue on to Srebrenica. They all screamed wildly at once. The Serb soldiers who sat slumped in their chairs looked on in amusement.

The eyes of the major accompanying the journalists darted to and fro in panic, as if looking for support, but most of the journalists had resigned themselves to the situation and hurried to reception to secure rooms. The major's shrill voice sounded above the din. He shouted pompously at the Serb commander that he would make an official protest. The man from the greetings programme stood behind him nodding violently.

The Serb said that he would personally guarantee that the journalists were conducted safely back to Tuzla. David asked tentatively if he could at least take the TV crews' equipment to the enclave. A dismissive gesture from the Serb commander silenced him.

The pungent smell of hundreds of hearths. It was the smell of war. Only a few hundred metres separated Tijmen from battalion headquarters in the hamlet of Potočari, on the northern edge of the enclave. The old battery factory, where the battalion was stationed, loomed out of the darkness. The smashed windows and flapping curtains gave the heavily shelled block of flats in the centre of the site a ghostly look. On the roof the blue UN flag waved proudly, powerfully lit by a bright lamp.

'This is the grim entrance,' Tijmen whispered to David.

They were briefly welcomed by Verbeek, then looked for a place to sleep. Together with David, Tijmen found an empty room on the first floor that most resembled a tiled bathroom. Someone called out in passing that the radiation level in the building was comparable to a measurement right in front of a colour TV. Tijmen was too tired to get worked up about that.

In the battalion staff quarters there had once been a laboratory. Later Henry was to tell him that after the local cleaners had thoroughly washed out the rooms he had given them new shoes. Their old ones had been eaten away by the corrosive battery acid.

In his room, together with David, he heated a tin of food on a burner. He took out the fork he always carried with him and tasted: white beans and pork. His stomach started rumbling.

Now that his initial excitement at their arrival had disappeared, Tijmen felt weary. After the meal he rolled his sleeping bag out next to David's, got undressed and lay down. He could smell his sweaty socks hanging over the chair. Just like French cheese. From tomorrow on he was going to wash his feet in cold water every day. At least if there *was* any water.

He listened to the rain outside and thought of his men in Brela: Jager, Jansen C., Jansen M., Kastelein... If he concentrated hard he could recite the whole list in alphabetical order. It was like counting sheep.

Even here on the first floor he could still hear the deep voice of Verbeek, Arend's high-pitched Hague accent, making jokes as always, and the men who brought the messages from the communications centre to battalion command in the ops room – the delicate play of pattering footsteps.

He had almost dozed off when an ear-splitting noise echoed through the tiled rooms. He sat bolt upright. David turned round.

'They're going to secure the command post with concrete slabs,' he muttered.

'Against incoming grenades,' he explained.

When Tijmen woke the next morning he found the enclave bathed in sunlight. There was no trace of snow. Spring must be early here. At breakfast he greeted old friends. You could scarcely call it a breakfast: for the time being they had to rely on French combat rations from the Canadians. He stuffed the boiled sweets into his pocket.

After breakfast he cheerfully climbed up the steps two at a time to the roof of the flats in the central compound. He stepped through the opening and screwed up his eyes in the bright light.

'Granddad!' yelled a voice.

He peered in annoyance in the direction of the sound. At the edge of the roof two soldiers were sitting with an aerial next to them. He screwed up his eyes into tiny slits. Then his face broke into a smile.

Frederik and Stefan constituted his own company's forward air control team, and had been sent out to Bosnia months before. He was about to say hello, but Frederik called out, 'Hold on a sec, Granddad, we've got to finish this job first.'

Tijmen took out his binoculars and scanned the terrain. Down below a patrol was jogging around the perimeter. The adjacent area was if anything even more dilapidated: he saw rusting oil drums and burnt out trucks. All the buildings were in ruins, as if a furious crowd had attacked them with sledgehammers. The houses across the road were not much better. Between these houses ran a mysterious path into the mountains. He followed its winding course until it disappeared round a bend.

Potočari nestled among the hills that tapered like a funnel towards the northern entrance to the enclave, in the direction of Yellow Bridge. Most hills were covered in dense beech woods, with a sheen of new foliage. It would not be long before nature exploded in the warm spring sunshine. Tijmen lowered the binoculars slightly and focused on observation post Papa, the border post with the outside world: their own Checkpoint Charlie.

Along the western side of the camp, right next to the fence, ran the enclave's only asphalted road. Tijmen peered southwards, towards Srebrenica, but a hill obscured the view. On the eastern side of the fence was a stream, the Guber. A pair of children chased each other along the bank and pulled faces at the patrol. The soldiers threw sweets across the water. Later someone told Tijmen that the Guber was both an open sewer and the enclave's water supply.

Beyond, meadows and fields sloped upwards. A few people were working the land, and half way up the hill was a cluster of farmhouses. A farmer was burning some branches. The thick smoke thrust up in a long column, until above the hills it was carried away on the wind. He followed the smoke with his binoculars and on one summit saw a Serb flag waving next to little figures like toy soldiers who, like him, were keeping a watch on the enclave through binoculars. Their shelters and trenches dominated the surroundings. The power of the Serbs over the valley was tangibly less. It was as if the farmer's smoke signals were saying: 'OK then, hit me if you can.'

'Watch it, Grandad,' yelled Frederik.

A moment later two jets passed over through the clear blue sky at high altitude.

'They'll be back again in just a moment.'

He listened to Stefan, who used the smoke in the field as a marker to guide the aircraft to the imaginary target. 'Windmill Alpha here, roger out.'

The jets came over again, much lower this time, roaring down the centre of the valley, and then climbed away steeply. At the highest point they fired three flares to mark the end of the exercise. The rockets made three long trails, until they disappeared as a dull glow against the sun, like fading fireworks.

'That'll have the Serbs shitting themselves,' shouted Frederik. 'We do this every day to keep sharp.'

'Weather permitting, that is,' added Stefan.

When the men had put away their equipment Tijmen told them cautiously that he wanted to be addressed by his own name from now on. He tried briefly to explain, but could feel the syllables getting caught in his teeth. He noticed to his annoyance that he spoke mainly to Frederik. Stefan would blindly follow everything that Frederik did. That was simply how the strict relations between officers and NCOs worked. As he was talking he saw the incomprehension in their eyes.

He went on talking to them for a while and could feel that the sun was already much stronger than he had expected. Frederik was in just a T-shirt.

That afternoon there was an incident. Verbeek's thundering voice reached the furthest corners of the building.

'And don't you think you can pull that one on me again!'

Downstairs in the corridor Tijmen bumped into two medical officers, who had just been thrown out of the CO's office. The older of the two, a major, explained.

'D-drove over a m-mine.'

The captain, who if anything was even paler than the major, extrapolated, 'Near O-P Echo. Map-reading error by him.'

He pointed accusingly at the major.

'At first w-we th-thought we-e w-were under fire. We t-turned the vehicle round and th-then we must have h-hit the second m-mine.'

'Bodywork pierced in twenty-nine places,' said the captain in a reedy voice.

'And what was up with him?' asked Tijmen, pointing in the direction of the CO.

'The old man was incandescent.'

They went on their way, shaking their heads.

As he watched them go, Tijmen wondered whether he would have done the same as Verbeek. He probably would. Setting an example, setting boundaries, that sort of thing.

The next morning David and Tijmen left for Srebrenica, where Bravo Company had set up camp.

The car zoomed across the asphalt. The fields were steaming in the morning sun. The faces of women, men and children popped up, especially those of children, with their famished eyes. Sometimes they called out, 'Mister, bombon?' As they opened a roll of sweets their eyes shone for a moment and they mouthed with thick accents 'Liquorice'. There were no fat people anywhere – all you saw were Mussulmen strolling down the road with an absent expression.

To the left, on a hill, a long trail of domestic waste spilled downwards. Tijmen had heard that the battalion had recently started burning rubbish. On more than one occasion people had hurt themselves retrieving a packet of biscuits or combat rations, or porn mags, which were worth a lot on the black market.

The car passed the wall of the abandoned football stadium, where all the wood had been stripped from the stands. On the wall there were slogans he could not decipher, alternating with Turkish crescents.

The town itself lay hidden deep in the valley like an extended ribbon. On top of one of the hills surrounding the town towered the mighty ruin of a castle. Next to it was a transmission mast.

It was busy in the city centre. People were everywhere: on the streets and ghostlike at the windows. Some gave thunderous looks at the white vehicle, most were too dazed to notice it. Each house was occupied by several families. Sometimes there were temporary extensions made of planks and plastic, with the letters UNHCR on them. The shelling, which had continued for two years, had left a trail of destruction. Virtually every house was pitted with small exploding stars, the devastating shrapnel from mortar rounds. The roads were strewn with craters in which the previous night's rain had collected.

The nerves of the inhabitants seemed equally shot to pieces. Quite a while ago these same people had flocked into this valley, like animals fleeing from a forest fire. A valley of stinking mud, the smell of decay, a ghetto.

Tijmen had little trouble imagining how the people here lived, how they bought candles in the market to light the cellars, how they boiled the polluted water to purify it, how they told their children about the war that would end one day...

Ejup Delalić walked down the road with his hands deep in the pockets of his parka. He hadn't even seen the vehicle that passed him. He was only nineteen, a refugee. The original inhabitants looked down on refugees, but he was young and found it easier to adapt than the others. One day, he had resolved, he would return to his village. It might take a year, or two, but he *would* go back. 'You sound just as angry and stubborn as those men on the radio,' said his father. His mother said little. For days on end she sat in an armchair in the unlit room only occasionally raising her voice for a glass of water or something to eat. 'Enjoying the twilight,' she called it. It was as if her skin were stretched taut over her bones. She wore her mother's floral dress, as if Granny's death were clinging to her. Her breasts had disappeared. Even when she went to bed she did not take off the dress, and when the siren wailed she refused to go into the cellar with the others.

They had been familiar voices, lads he had been at school with. The old neighbour had come to warn them. They had lowered the shutters in front of the windows and spent the first night in the cellar. It had stunk of fresh faeces. The earth shook. The village was already under fire. In the following days the shelling had got heavier and heavier.

For a moment there had been a glimmer of hope. Muslim fighters had control of the dam on the Drina and were threatening to blow it up. But the dam had not been destroyed, the 'Četniks' had mopped up the resistance and attacked the country like a tidal wave.

On the third evening the shelling seemed to subside. He had gone upstairs. Through a chink he had seen the men marching into the street. Men in black balaclavas. 'We are crusaders against Islam,' they had sung. They searched the houses with torches. His father, his little brother and he had fled out of the back door and hidden among the rocks behind the shed. They had quickly gathered some loose branches and pulled them over themselves.

The soldiers had moved further into the village. There were shots. A little later black clouds of smoke rose from the direction of the mosque. Then they had come back. They had driven the women and children from the houses. Ejup had heard everything.

He remembered exactly what his little sister had been wearing that day: purple plastic shoes, tight jeans and a thick red sweater. Later everyone had their own version of events, but he, Ejup, had seen everything.

The women were herded together next to their houses, mothers protecting their daughters. His sister had been singled out. They wanted her to tell them where the men were. She had given nothing away. She had been shot, just like that. Sabiha was fourteen.

'We're going to make some Serbs,' the men had said. The youngest girls were picked out and taken to the woods. 'If you cry, we'll finish you off right away,' said the 'Četniks'. Hours later the girls had come back, their faces black and blue. They did not cry but were deathly still. Yes, they were deathly still. Some could scarcely stand up.

Finally the 'Četniks' left. The villagers had emerged from their hiding place. Everyone was looking for everyone. People were yelling names through the night. They had quickly gathered some things from the house and put vegetables and potatoes in sacks. His father had divided people into groups, family by family. When a family had too few men, he added some. He had sketched out on a piece of paper the route they must take. They hadn't possessed any papers, and didn't even know where the front was. Only later had he discovered that there *was* no front.

First they had hidden in the woods for a few hours. On the edge of the village a man was screaming in his death agony – he had been skewered like a pig on a spit. His father had gone back to put the man out of his misery. Then they had set off, at first keeping to the west bank of the Drina, then straight through the hills to Srebrenica. Night after night they had walked and walked like hunted foxes. They had passed Muslim villages that had been burned to the ground by the 'Četniks', and Serb villages that had been gutted by Muslims. Sometimes there was the sound of rifle fire in the distance. En route people whispered, 'The "Četniks" take no prisoners.'

Ejup took a deep breath. Once he had had plans, an aim. He could no longer talk to his parents. Their lethargy got on his nerves. Every morning after breakfast he fled the house and wandered the streets. This morning he had told his parents what he was going to do, 'I'm going to fight for Mustafa. If you want to let yourselves be slaughtered, that's up to you.'

In front of Bravo Company's gate there was quite a crowd, which slowly gave way when the driver beeped. The sentry pushed the people back with the butt of his rifle and shut the iron gate with large padlocks. Tijmen felt like a spectator and witness at the same time.

Eddy greeted them with the exhausting cheerfulness that Tijmen knew so well. He feigned a laugh, but felt a wave of anger go through him when Eddy showed him his new headed notepaper. The heading read:

    Bravo/Bull Company Dutchbat
    'First In'

That was a lie: the company of engineers had arrived much earlier. Eddy had got used to dropping references in passing to that new status: the first company to arrive in Srebrenica. In Tijmen he had at last found a sucker from Alpha Company. The illustrious Alphas, Verbeek's chosen ones. Tijmen saw Eddy's smile, the infuriating smile of a deeply satisfied man.

A little later Tijmen was in the Bravo Company bar. David had brought two cups of coffee and gave one to him. Just the smell made him feel sick.

'Have you heard?' asked David.

Tijmen bit the rim of his cup. David told him about the argument between Cees and Eddy, and the slanging match at their morning discussion. Eddy was paying less and less attention to the orders of the major from battalion headquarters.

'And to think that Cees is still protecting him.'

Tijmen looked at him questioningly.

'You really don't know, do you?'

David told him that Eddy had agreed a bet with a Ukrainian officer. Cees had acted as referee during the arm wrestling. The Ukrainian had won easily. Eddy, who was roaring drunk, drew his pistol and put it to his opponent's temple. In a slurred voice he had yelled, 'Shall I pull the trigger?' When Cees had tried to tug his arm away Eddy yelled, 'It's not loaded.' Later Cees had found Eddy outside, lying in the mud. He carefully removed the weapon from his hand. When he drew back the slide there was a gleaming copper-coloured round in the chamber.

'But Cees didn't breath a word of this to the CO,' said David in conclusion.

'That's very big of him,' said Tijmen, as if he heard such things every day.

Eddy elbowed his way between the soldiers.

'Too late, too late,' he cried in Tijmen's direction.

The words hit Tijmen smack in the face like a football, and went on stinging. He froze. David must have seen his confusion and hastily told Eddy about their short stay in Lukavac, but Tijmen scarcely heard. He nudged David.

'Let's go and see Harold.'

The draught from the stairwell brought with it the voices of the drunken Canadians, who were celebrating their departure upstairs. In the cellar all daylight had been shut out. Tijmen inhaled the stale air, his gaze focused on the two shaky beams supporting the ceiling. The braces holding the concrete ceiling together had deep-brown rust spots on them, and sandbags were piled against a steel door. The small windows just under the ceiling were strengthened with sandbags on the outside. On one wall, which was covered with a pale green film of mould, was a large map of the whole enclave, on which the location of the observation posts was indicated with pins. They were in a circle around the enclave, exactly on the line of the border with the Bosnian Serbs, which was marked on the map as a thick red line.

The cellar under the Bravo Company base was full of the occupants' laundry. Stretchers were pushed close together and even in the aisle there was scarcely room to move, since the equipment strewn throughout the cellar blocked one's passage on all sides. In a corner there was a concrete staircase leading upstairs. Right next to this staircase there was a table with the occupants' cooking equipment, and next to it a cabinet crammed with combat rations. A single bulb dangled loose on a wire and shed a faint light over the men.

'The Muslim commander is Mustafa Avdić, former bodyguard of the Serb president. For reasons that are not clear he was dismissed from that job and in 1991 became a policeman in Potočari. Calls himself general, receives his orders direct from Sarajevo and controls virtually all trade in Srebrenica. No, let's face it, he controls *all* trade.'

Tijmen studied the face of the man who was dishing up the information in a staccato voice, Harold, the intelligence officer. He had known Harold for years, but actually knew little about him. Oh yes, that his wife had told him that he mustn't call her a nurse, but a nursing expert. Harold, who had played the lead in the recruitment film for the airmobile brigade; he had pestered the director until he was the only one allowed to record some words. The sound man had taken Harold to a secluded spot. Harold must have recorded it ten times: 'Look, men, the bridge.' When the clip was first shown on TV, they had all watched. Harold was centre shot. He pointed to the bridge, and if you watched closely you could see him say soundlessly, 'Look, men, the bridge.'

A little way away sat Cornelissen, Harold's driver, listening in intently. He had travelled ahead of the battalion with Harold. They had been camping out in the cellar for over a month.

'At the beginning of the war Mustafa lured thirteen Serb policemen into an ambush in Potočari...'

Harold turned to his listeners with mounting enthusiasm.

'In the first year of the war he and his fighters went on the rampage in the surrounding Serb villages. He looted the houses mercilessly and carried off the stolen goods to Srebrenica. The bodies of the victims were also brought back and dragged through the streets on meat hooks.'

He paused for a moment to heighten the dramatic effect of his words, and to tell from their faces that he had their attention. As if he, Harold, was the spider in the middle of its web. They were dependent on him for all their information.

'Mustafa's cruelty knew no bounds,' he went on. 'He didn't even shrink from cutting the heads off the corpses and displaying them impaled on poles in front of the *opština*. The Muslim commander was feared from Skelani on the Drina to the suburbs of Tuzla.'

He indicated the size of the area with his pointer.

'He usually attacked the villages on Serb feast days, when people least expected it. Shall I tell you what Mustafa looks like?'

'Go ahead,' said Tijmen.

'He can lift you up with one hand. He's wrestling champion of the enclave, a real super-fit type.'

The listeners stared at Harold.

'No shit,' he said, 'I mean it, every word is true. You should see this Mustafa.'

'Don't let us stop you,' said David dryly.

'Where was I,' said Harold. 'Right, Mustafa then. Discussions with him often last for hours and the drink flows freely. Never talk to him about history, because then it will take even longer, then it'll get into the Roman and Byzantine Empires, the Austro-Hungarian Empire and of course the Second World War with Četniks, Hitler and Ustašas.'

Any minute now Harold would be saying that they had to address Mustafa as 'General'. He must love going about with the Muslim commander almost every day, so as to be out of the oppressive cellar for a while.

Harold concluded his story. Tijmen breathed a sigh of relief. That was over: he had been brought nicely up to speed again. He knew all about Mustafa, but he could only guess about the identity of the Serbs.

On the way back to Potočari, Tijmen looked for Mustafa's face among those at the side of the road, but they all seemed the same kind of Musselmen who populated the streets on the way to Srebrenica. An old woman stroked her grandchild's hair. Perhaps it was her child. Ages were almost impossible to establish here.

It was David who first broke the silence.

'We'd better stay on the right side of that Mustafa.'

'I'm not sure,' said Tijmen, and told David briefly of his doubts.

'You don't like him, do you?'

'Who? Mustafa?'

'No, Harold.'

'He's OK,' said Tijmen.

Three days later the company sergeant major of Alpha Company appeared in the compound. Not many people got on with the CSM, but Tijmen had a good relationship with Herman. He sometimes told Herman he liked him, which helped him come out of his shell. Last autumn Herman had even brought him a box of chanterelles. Tijmen thought it best not to say that he didn't cook.

Herman was stiff when other people were around. There were a considerable number of people from Twente in the company. They called themselves the 'Twente Association', and hung around with each other, but Herman, who hailed from Twente, was never among them. Tijmen had sometimes wondered why that was. Perhaps it was because of Herman's appearance: he was a short chap with a beard, not exactly the figure of a tough guy, more a strapping gnome.

Herman was the most experienced soldier in the company and had been CSM for five years. 'I've worn down three company commanders,' he always said. But the one who was worn down most was Herman. He had been sent out before to Lebanon with UNIFIL. Only when he talked about his leave in Tel-Aviv did his eyes light up for a moment. He called it Screw City.

With Herman, Tijmen visited the observation posts in the mountains that they were going to take over from Bravo Company. The atmosphere was worlds removed from that in town. Often the observation posts were in the vicinity of hushed villages where chickens ran about in the street and people gave you a friendly nod. Splendid panoramas loomed up at almost every corner, with one hill appearing behind another in every shade of green. There was often a blanket of thin mist draped over the roofs, motionless: a mist through which echoed the morning prayers from a minaret.

Farmers were even still working in the fields adjoining the border of the enclave. How much courage did it take to venture within Serb firing range every day? And the people of the enclave had had to surrender their weapons.

Along the donkey paths that linked the posts, 'MINES' was sometimes written in the sand. Many times they had to retrace their footsteps back down the path, and occasionally they came upon freshly dug graves.

In the observation posts Tijmen sensed hostility from the men of Bravo Company. Was this Eddy's sweet revenge on the Alphas? Tijmen kept thinking of what the padre had told him, 'There are videos in circulation of local women and our soldiers.' They came up against a wall of silence and suspicion. At least, that was how Tijmen was to remember it later.

The following week, while Herman got the hall in order for billeting the soldiers, Tijmen wrote out his plans. It surprised him how he had resigned himself to his lot. He preferred to spend days alone, on top of the block or at the back of the compound, where people hardly ever went. Inside, the dichotomy that had him in its grip continued to rage: a mixture of a longing for excitement and a crushing feeling of futility.

And yet he began to feel almost at home in the besieged enclave. In the evenings he wrote in his diary. He still had oceans of time before his men arrived.

Hadija Ibrahimović was a charming petite girl with long wavy copper-blond hair, a smiling mouth with bright-red lips, freckles and fierce dark eyes. 'Enchanting eyes', people said. None of the other cleaners wore lipstick. It had cost her a fortune, and almost as much trouble as getting a job with the Dutch.

Some clicked their tongues when she went past. Others tried to make eye contact. But Hadija always lowered her eyes, too shy to look back. Every time she said, 'In the kingdom of the blind the one-eyed man is king.'

She hated her work. She had never had to clean at home, where her mother did all the work, and her father had never taken her to task about it. She was the apple of his eye, and it was he who had made it possible for her to study in Sarajevo with a scholarship, while her mother had always said that she must marry a rich man from the city. It was her father who before she left had said, 'I'm jealous of you.'

In the Bosnian capital a whole new world had opened up for her: the old town with its bazaar – the Baščaršija – the Habsburg quarters with their wide avenues, the theatre she loved going to, the library where it was always quiet and cool, full of books she had never read. And friends; for the first time she danced in Nikes, high on alcohol.

During the lectures she had absorbed knowledge as if life depended on it. She was a chosen one. No one from her village was at university. Her aim was to become a doctor, and she had resolved to pay her debt of honour and work as a GP in her native region.

She had always been different from the others. She had known from a very early age that she was a loner. The village lads were actually rather intimidated by her haughty beauty. If her parents had given her anything it was her sense that she was unique, as if touched by divine power. The other children had always teased her. She couldn't have cared less. She, Hadija, was going to be someone.

When she returned to Bajramovići after her first semester in Sarajevo she had told her father she was no longer going to wear a headscarf. To her amazement he agreed and from that moment on she wore her hair loose. But since she had been working for the Dutch she had put it up again and fixed it with the only hairclip she still possessed. 'Long hair is unhygienic,' the sergeant-major had told her, as if she didn't know that herself.

The war had devastated her future, carved up the country into 'them and us'. First there were the stories about Dubrovnik then they were supplanted by those about Vukovar. Not long after that, the barricades went up and Sarajevo was divided into ethnic zones. The Croat and Serb students missed class more and more often and the same process of elimination took place among the lecturers, most of whom disappeared to Belgrade. From that moment they were 'all Muslims together'. It was the beginning of the end. After a short vacation at home it had proved impossible to travel back to Sarajevo.

Hadija wondered if she would ever get away from the enclave. What she found most unbearable of all was the stench. The smell, – a grainy body odour – that got into your clothes and did not even disappear after thorough washing. It was mainly that smell that incorporated you with the lost souls, even more than poverty and the daily humiliation of the work. But she couldn't even talk to anyone about that: people wouldn't understand. She should be glad she *had* work.

If she ever did become a doctor she would choose a place as far away as possible from the enclave. And if she earned lots of money she would send for her father and mother and little brothers. Perhaps she would go to the Dalmatian coast, where her father had owned a summer house. Or had the war reached those places too? She must ask the sergeant-major sometime.

Now all she had were her study books, which she sat reading intently every evening anew. At least, if there was light. She knew whole chunks off by heart.

When the cleaners entered the building in the mornings and Tijmen heard Hadija's voice, a little higher, above the others, it made him feel dizzy. There was something mysterious about her. It had something to do with her smile.

Soon he knew exactly what time she would appear in the corridor. Every morning anew: he, leaning in the doorway, and the girl nodding in greeting. He looked forward to those meetings, but she didn't come any closer. The language barrier was too great, time was too short and apart from that it was as if she respected his solitude. What they had to say to each other remained unspoken.

He wouldn't say a word to her. It had been drummed into him before he left: 'Fraternising with "locals" is strictly forbidden'. No one knew the knot he got in his stomach when he heard that word. 'Locals'... it sounded like a type of animal.

No soldiers from Alpha Company had arrived yet. Lex too was still en route with his Charlie Company. Tijmen found some distraction in the scavenging expeditions he organised with Herman. There was plenty of wood in the tall flats. Competition had arisen among the staff for desks that were intact. The billeting hall was being cleared under Herman's supervision, and even the construction of the company command post right next to the mess was making steady progress.

Tijmen had wondered with increasing frequency these days where on earth Eddy's hostility came from. Yes, it was true, he, Tijmen, was Verbeek's blue-eyed boy and what's more, commander of Alpha King's Company in which according to tradition Prince Willem – later to become King William III – had served in the nineteenth century. The only company that carried its own standard: the Prince Alexander Fanion, in memory of the prince of that name who had died young and also been a grenadier, while Bravo Company had to make do with the bull mascot, because, so the story went, the deputy company commander at some time in the 1950s liked going to Spain for his holidays.

Tijmen whistled softly to himself, and then sang the words he vaguely remembered:

> Peat in your backpack,
> peat in your backpack,
> straw's old-fashioned nowadays.
> Peat in your backpack,
> peat in your knapsack,
> now your head must be well raised.

It was the Regimental March of the Grenadiers, which could only be played if a company of grenadiers or chasseurs were taking part in a march past. But actually that didn't mean very much. The transformation of the armoured infantry battalion into an airmobile unit in 1992 had been the coup de grâce for the grenadier tradition. For years they had prepared for a confrontation with the Russians and the combat manual had been their Bible, their certainty, with annually repeated exercises and tests. After a while he could do them in his sleep. But now the grenadiers were red-berets, special to the Dutch airmobile unit, elite troops who could be deployed anywhere in the world. He had learned how to 'rig' Land Rovers, how to hang them under helicopters. He had learned that you could use a hook to discharge the static electricity generated by the rotor blades. It hadn't been much good to him. Before they had been sent out, the armoured personnel carriers they had just decommissioned had been returned.

'We are the chosen ones,' said Tijmen softly to himself.

At the annual regimental dinners of the grenadier officers there was invariably talk of an almost open hostility between the old Indies veterans and the young 'airmobile' officers serving with the battalion, who had grandiose ideas about their new status.

The anniversary of the regiment was still celebrated every year on 7 July and the Indies veterans were still regularly to be seen: at their reunions they visited the monument in the barracks. At the time when Brokkel was CO the tradition was held in high esteem, more than that: it was the backbone of everything. For the first six months new officers were ignored in the mess and had to wear the red insignia of the line regiments instead of the yellow-and-red ones with the grenadiers' grenade. Every officer had to have a small red Watneys badge, the emblem of the British brewery, and if it could not be produced, the penalty was a round in the mess.

Tijmen remembered how few real grenadier officers were left. Lex was proud of his past as a commando and was more a green-beret than a red one. Eddy had transferred as a captain from the artillery and even Verbeek was a 'Sudeten grenadier', having begun his service long ago as a Limburg chasseur. Only David and Tijmen had been assigned to the grenadiers straight out of RMA, taken their oath before the standard in 1986 and never left. That was becoming more and more of a rarity. He tried to find other names. Manus definitely, Henry perhaps, but he wasn't so sure.

How far removed he felt from that grenadier past with the famous standard! The standard with the inscriptions: 'Ten-Day Campaign', 'Ypenburg 1940-Ockenburg 1940', 'West Java 1946-1949' and 'East Java 1947-1949'. Once he had attached a lot of importance to being assigned to Her Majesty's Guards regiment.

'The afore-mentioned regiment of Grenadiers shall be composed of a select number of officers and men, and assignment to the same must be considered a distinction, an honour and a dispensation and regarded as a reward for good service.'

It was Herman and Tijmen's last evening in the enclave. Alpha Company's mission had been changed yet again. It was to be the only company in the battalion not to be based in Srebrenica but at Tuzla Airbase. On the first floor of the staff building a farewell party for Herman and Tijmen was underway.

Bouma, the Regimental Sergeant Major, came in, surveyed the scene and left immediately. Arend said, 'He looks flabbergasted.' It didn't stop him from continuing his demonstration.

He was describing the CO's daughters. The spectators did not need a great deal of imagination. Everyone knew how they had looked at the presentation of the red berets: their mini-skirts had given everyone a view of their panties. They were white.

Squatting there on the ground Arend looked just like a wild ape, licking his lips with his tongue. In between, he yelled lines that seemed to come straight out of his extensive collection of porn. Arend had photocopied a letter asking all his friends and acquaintances for 'dirty books'. Whenever mail arrived there were always letters for Arend.

'Hey, Jungs! Fick meine Pussy mit ihren durchtrainierten Riemen, und ich mach ein Paar Blas-übungen mit ihren Schwanzen.'

If Cees had not told him that part of Alpha Company was already on its way to Tuzla Airbase in two convoys, Tijmen would definitely have left the room. Now he stayed put and smiled sourly. That afternoon Eddy had talked of Tuzla Airbase as if it were a consolation prize. At that moment Speedy was supposed to be receiving orders on behalf of Tijmen at Nordbat.

Arend caught the imaginary sperm on his tongue and rolled his eyes. The spectators cheered.

The bottle of rakija was half-empty, and Tijmen could feel the alcohol going to his head. It was the first time he had drunk rakija, a spirit that caught fire if you held a match to it. At first he wanted hold on to the intoxication that had taken over his head, in order to muffle his rage; the feeling that his body was sliding out from underneath him. But now the anger was compacting again, like a huge block at the back of his head. He had tried all afternoon to get hold of Verbeek, but he was touring the enclave with the commander-in-chief. And this evening he mustn't be disturbed, as he was writing a diary for the newspapers.

Herman looked on edge and fragile, paler and more brittle than ever. The news that the plans for Alpha Company had been changed yet again that afternoon had hit him, if anything, even harder than Tijmen. Herman's moody character had taken over his personality. It was the same moodiness that made the men in the company hate him.

'And didn't they say anything else?' asked Herman.

'Nothing,' said Tijmen, 'except that from now on we'll be under the command of Nordbat. They'll have to sort it out, they said in the ops room.'

'The dirty rotten bastards!' shouted Herman.

Arend left the room to go to the toilet. When he came back he hissed, 'The RSM is eavesdropping in the corridor.'

'Sod the RSM,' whispered Tijmen. 'The prick,' he added loudly.

Herman smiled.

From the corridor came the sound of rapid footsteps.

The following morning as they were leaving Tijmen felt his own cool detachment. It was an effort to respond to Verbeek's friendly grin. He looked for David's face among the others but couldn't find it.

The wheels of the vehicles crunched and the convoy got underway, puffing and squeaking. Slowly the lead vehicle left the compound. Verbeek watched it go with a worried look. Tijmen turned his head away. In the distance stood the girl; he didn't know her name, but their eyes met for a second.

The sun shone and it rained. A rainbow circled the enclave.

PART IV
DANCING ON A COLD TILED FLOOR

After Tijmen left Srebrenica in mid-March 1994 the ways had parted for his company and the rest of the battalion. Alpha Company first carried out operations at Tuzla Airbase and later in the 'Sapna Thumb'. These locations were not worlds removed from the Srebrenica enclave, but physically there was an almost unbridgeable gap. The Serbs ruled the area in between.

The psychological distance between the enclave in Eastern Bosnia and the rest of the Muslim area in the centre of the country was, if anything, even greater. Srebrenica was a 'safe haven', where the population had to be protected from the Serb aggressor by UN troops. But on the borders of Central Bosnia there was a continual war raging between the Muslims and Serbs which the UN could do little more than observe.

Just as Alpha Company had been separated from the rest of the battalion, Tijmen and David had been split up. Not until their return to the Netherlands, at the end of July 1994, did they see each other again. Tijmen had served another six months or so with the airmobile unit in the Netherlands, but the exercises he took part in failed to evoke any semblance of reality in him and in February 1995 he left the army. Afterwards he had holed up in his flat for months.

It was July 1995. David had already said on the telephone that he couldn't make it too late, but had come straight to the pub in Korenmarkt, one of the main squares in town, when Tijmen rang.

David took the two glasses the waitress had brought from the bar.

'Have you heard?' asked David.

Tijmen nodded. There was something conspiratorial about their meeting. Srebrenica had fallen. An unstoppable stream of rumours had started flowing. The Minister of Overseas Development had already talked of thousands of dead. He had used the word genocide.

'We all knew this could happen,' said David, 'a year ago, when I was there. It doesn't surprise me one bit.'

For a second Tijmen felt a hint of painful affinity with the men who were now in Bosnia: soldiers of Dutchbat, airmobile, red-beret, blue-beret. But the affinity was no longer really there. The last CO of Dutchbat had failed hopelessly. There was only David left. The one person he still saw, a last link with his past.

Tijmen almost blurted out, 'The reports attract me and repel me at the same time. I follow everything, but at times it all gets too much for me and there are days I don't want to know any more, when I throw the Army newspaper, which is still delivered, straight in the bin.'

David shook his head and bent forward towards the notebook Tijmen had put on the table.

March 1994

Zlata Sarić strode on in the direction of the main gate. She gripped her bag firmly under her right armpit.

It had begun with one loaf. It was even easier than she had thought. She crept in early in the morning when there was no one in the kitchen. And every morning the baskets stood there unguarded. Sometimes she grabbed a few apples and once, after she had walked round the whole building to see if the coast was clear, she had filled a pan with soup. It was a long time since she had tasted such thick tomato soup. She felt no shame; there was food in abundance at the airbase. During the day she hid her hoard in one of the empty huts in the middle of the camp. Only when she had finished her work as a cleaner in the main building did she hurry back to her hiding place. No one had ever asked what she was doing in this part of the camp.

In the distance she heard the bus. Zlata quickened her step, holding the bag a little more firmly under her arm. Her jet-black hair swayed as she walked, and her plump face shone with the effort, her heavy make-up covered with pearly sweat drops. She dallied for a moment. The bus pulled up at the gate with a hiss and Zlata walked quickly past it. The Dutch boarded on the other side of the bus; since they had taken over from the handful of Swedes, the bag checks had increased.

She turned right. Only when she had disappeared completely behind the bushes did she breathe a sigh of relief and look back. In the distance the rear lights of the bus disappeared towards Tuzla.

It took her fifty minutes to walk home to Tojšići. Sometimes she was given a lift on a farm cart, first, on the road through the open fields where the crops had been ailing for whole seasons, then the wide asphalted road, which in the past had been used as an extra runway for the airbase, and was pitted with holes made by Serb grenades. Not one of the wrecked cars the Swedes had put there earlier remained. The road was now blocked with huge obstacles filled with stones. These blockades were the result of a mysterious agreement to placate the 'Četniks', so it was whispered. Only the main runway of the airbase was fit for use. She stopped for a moment and took a mirror out of her bag. She spat on her thumb and touched up her makeup.

At a stall at the T-junction, she traded one of the loaves for a bottle of Coca-Cola; the stall where you could still buy everything, at exorbitant prices. Coca-Cola, Marlboro, fresh fruit and washing-up liquid: that was luxury.

A quarter of an hour later she had reached her house. She threw the bag on the table.

'Emir, are you home yet?'

No reaction. There was no one to be seen on the factory site across the road. Nor was there any sign of her Emir, who was one of the few men with a job. There must be another offensive imminent. The woman next door, who spoke German, was working in the garden. Her Serb husband had not returned from Germany. Zlata remembered having once asked her why she hadn't left too. 'Warten,' she had said, 'nur warten.'

In the kitchen she displayed the items: three loaves and a bottle of lemonade. She hadn't even heard Emir come in. He crept towards her without making a sound. Zlata let out a shriek. Emir looked at the work top and pressed a kiss in the nape of her neck.

'I wrote down these stories in the evenings,' said Tijmen.

Without a word David took two new glasses from the waitress.

'No one knew about it. In the evenings I created my own world.'

'And during the day?' asked David.

'During the day I played the King of Tuzla.'

'To the king!' toasted David.

Two men sat down at the table next to theirs. Touché was the only pub that David and he sometimes went to: their old local in the centre of Arnhem. David had changed: he'd become calmer, more thoughtful. As always in summer there was a red glow on his skin, which shone with ointment. He suffered from a skin complaint and on hot summer days it always lay in waiting, ready to erupt. This disease made David's appearance even more rugged, as if the grooves in his face had been etched all the deeper. And yet there was still something boyish about him.

Suddenly there were thoughts of another summer, long ago. Tijmen had bumped into David on the parade ground, his swollen skin covered in ulcers. Only after much insistence had he agreed to tell the doctor. 'Just for you,' David had finally relented.

At last Tijmen could tell someone what had got into him. It had a strange attraction that surprised him.

'And so within a day of our farewell party in Srebrenica, I suddenly found myself at Tuzla Airbase.'

In flickering film images the base lay spread out before Tijmen. It was definitely going to be a beautiful day. It was raining, but the sun was making strenuous efforts to break through the clouds.

He started the jeep and pulled onto the road, leaving behind him the wood where the company's quarters were. At the kitchen one of the cooks waved to him. His hand went automatically to his beret.

For two days his company had been under the command of Nordbat, the Norwegian-Danish-Swedish battalion that had been billeted around Tuzla, initially for a period of two weeks. Who could say whether it would stop at that? Links with the battalion in Srebrenica had been temporarily severed. Just as well: from now on he was more or less his own boss. He was king, King of Tuzla.

Hadn't the commander said that he, Tijmen, was in command at night? He was filled with a modest feeling of pride. For the time being the commander was sleeping at the Tuzla Hotel. He chuckled. The men had dubbed the Norwegian airforce colonel 'Tom Cruise'.

The car shot across the dark-grey apron and then turned left onto the runway. He cast a quick glance into the distance at the hostile Viz Mountain, where the Serbs had their positions. 'Sugar Hill', the Swedes called it. With rapid movements he steered the vehicle deftly from left to right across the gleaming asphalt. The tyres screeched: little chance of them hitting him.

Along the whole south-eastern side of the base there was no sign of a fence. In the distance were dark hills, clad in the green of dense pinewoods. This evening he would send an armoured personnel carrier, YPR, to this side of the camp to deter intruders. He had seen on the news how they dubbed the YPR a 'tank'. He scoffed at the paradoxical nature of his mission: securing the airbase in order to ensure the supply of aid meant principally 'keeping the population out'.

The radio crackled: 'Romeo here, I'm leaving the runway.'

He passed the munitions storage and the hangars which had once housed the planes of the Yugoslav air force. Between two of the hangars was a wrecked aircraft, stranded on its belly. A red star still adorned the broken tail. This had once been the largest airbase in Yugoslavia. Someone had told him that there had been five runways.

He stopped at one of the observation posts built by the Swedes, got out and climbed the steps. 'All alone, Drent?'

'Kolenbrander's gone for a crap.'

Drent handed him his plastic UN mug. There were the remnants of soup round the rim. He turned the cup round and sipped his tea. From here there was a good view of the road to the village, of all the traffic to and from the east where the front was. Not far away a few boys were practising basketball shots. On the other side the base stretched out, largely obscured from view by the woods behind the hangars.

Kolenbrander climbed the steps and joined them. Tijmen listened to the impact of mortar rounds to the north-east. How stultifyingly dull it must be for the men to note every strike, often miles away. There wasn't much point in the task: no trace was found of it in the evening situation reports. Only if the airbase itself came under fire was there a slight chance that it would be noticed at headquarters in Kiseljak.

'Did you see that, Cap?'

Drent pointed down. At the base of the tower the sandbags were torn. Tijmen made a note. Together with the repairs to the fence, these tasks would be quite a job. What's more, only part of his force had arrived. The rest were still in the hotel in Brela on the Croatian coast, and would follow on later.

He put his notebook away, put his hand on the banister of the steps and slid down. Over his shoulder he called out, 'Just let the doctor know, I'm on my way.'

The medical field post consisted of two cheerful brick buildings at the centre of the airbase. The doctor was already outside waiting. Oscar looked almost as young as the soldiers for whom he was responsible. The only thing that distinguished him was his straight hair. He wore it slightly longer than his soldiers, just over his ears, with a large lock at the front that he kept tossing back with a brief movement of his head. He looked like an English public schoolboy.

The doc proudly showed him his new territory. It smelled of disinfectant. The 'shock room' had already been prepared for any disasters, in the sickbay there were six neatly made-up field beds next to each other, and one of the buildings even had a bunker. The room was lined with thick wooden beams and the walls and ceiling were reinforced with three layers of sandbags.

Soon Tijmen was standing with water splashing down on his body. This was the only really good shower in the whole camp. There were four others in the company's quarters. Showering was a privilege. Showering was your only privacy. 'Shoot one-handed,' said the doc always, 'that prevents injuries.' He also said, 'Did you know that two percent of men can suck themselves off?'

After visiting the field hospital Tijmen drove to the back gate. He tore past the main building and bumped along the road bordered on both sides by the minefield overgrown with bushes, then along the semi-hardened road that ran past the runway while mud splashed left and right.

'Romeo here, I'm on the A1,' he shouted into the radio, using the codename.

He stopped briefly at the back gate, noted that there was only one row of sandbags on the roof of the observation post, saluted Vink and left. On the way back he passed the forest where the villagers of Gornje Dubrave chopped their wood every day. The forest too was full of mines, a legacy of the Bosnian government army and the Bosnian Serbs who had in turn controlled the base. All over the airbase grenades and mines were still sticking out of the ground. Yesterday they had found one two metres behind their sleeping quarters. 'Only the asphalt road is safe,' Speedy had said. 'There are still thousands of them about.'

Two days later, for the first time since he had been sent out, Tijmen had a chance to have a lie in. He had the whole morning ahead of him and didn't know what to do with it.

Outside the sun was shining, but the room was damp and bitterly cold. The old dilapidated living quarters of the Yugoslav air force still had no water or light and the thick walls kept spring at bay. On the ground floor a temporary bar had been set up where, with the help of an aggregator that thoroughly disturbed his sleep, a coffee-maker bubbled away for the guard coming on or going off duty.

From further along the corridor came the voices of Herman and Speedy. They were talking about Speedy's wife and 'the little one'. Tijmen had met Yvonne a few times. She had been born on a travellers' site. Not that she had told him this herself. He knew from Speedy. During parties in the mess she was avoided by the officers, and especially by their wives. Yvonne was the only one wearing an evening dress with lots of white lace, the same for every party. For this reason Speedy also tended to be cold-shouldered.

Tijmen had never talked to him about it. He did know, though, that his deputy had been cadet battalion commander at the RMA and had been to the renowned Barlaeus Gymnasium. Speedy had once said to him, 'My father was a baker. I was the only one in my class whose father was a baker.'

The voices moved away. The first platoon led by Niels had meanwhile left for a small village thirty-five kilometres distant, on the road to Brčko, in the north. They were securing the compound of a Swedish company that had been transferred in great haste to Mount Igman near Sarajevo. Tijmen realised that there was already something of an estrangement between the soldiers of the first platoon and the rest of the company, just as a rift had opened up between Alpha Company and the battalion in Srebrenica on the other side of the Serb-controlled area.

Verbeek had rung yesterday evening, for the first time. He would probably be coming for Easter, which he had said as if conferring a favour. He also talked of a possible mission in the 'Sapna Thumb'. When Verbeek had said in passing that Frank Platvoet, the deputy CO, would be stationed with the company, Tijmen felt the rage taking over. Fortunately the CO had added that he would retain command. Tijmen had acted as if none of it was of much interest to him.

Yesterday too the first plane had finally landed, carrying the Secretary-General's personal representative. The small Japanese chap had made an impression of nervousness. The base was at a high pitch of excitement: 'pomp and circumstance'. With a bit of luck it would have been shown yesterday evening on CNN.

The Japanese had made a passionate speech about the importance of the opening for the supply of aid. But nothing had been said about the Serbs' refusal to allow this. Serb radio had already spoken of American 'special forces' that had supposedly landed at the airbase.

Tijmen walked to the window and opened it a fraction. Down below in the road a couple of local civilian staff members were working with brooms and plastic bags. 'There are already about two hundred of them working at the base,' Speedy had said.

Tijmen rummaged in the bag under his chair.

'Eddy or Lex might equally well have been sent to Tuzla Airbase with their companies,' ventured David. 'What's so special about that?'

'Equally well?' Tijmen repeated, putting a new pack of papers on the table. 'Quite the contrary, Verbeek chose me especially because he had most confidence in me and my company. He told me that later.'

'There's nothing wrong with that,' said David.

'Obviously I played my role with conviction,' said Tijmen, raising his voice. 'To begin with I was quite proud that I had been chosen, but in those two and a half months on Tuzla Airbase I had the sneaking feeling that Alpha Company had been forgotten by the battalion. The Swedish paid scarcely any attention to us either. Even the meetings I had to attend were conducted largely in Swedish. Of course I was glad to be my own boss, and I was also finally rid of the rivalry with Eddy and Lex and their companies, but that couldn't remove the sense of abandonment. I filled scores of pages in my diary, recording the story. I've never given them to anyone to read before.'

Tijmen pushed the papers towards David.

Friday, 25 March 1994

There are aircraft landing every day, but almost all of them are empty. Their arrival is mainly symbolic.

Today there were UN teddy bears on sale in the bar. They fit exactly into the cardboard postal packs that we send home, and had sold out within the hour. I sent one to my godson. In five days' time a two-year-old in Holland will open a parcel from Tim. He can already say that, 'Tim'. It was one of the first things he could say. And when he sees soldiers on TV, he shouts 'Tim'. At least, so my sister writes. And he's started calling tanks 'cranes'.

Tuesday, 5 April 1994

Grimaces, faces closer to tears than laughter; still they try, with a weird leer.

On their way to the meeting at the airbase, somewhere between the first platoon's compound and Tuzla, Niels and Corporal De Wet came across a woman hit by a stray mortar round. They muttered something about a skull half blown away and 'the left eye hanging out'. On the way to the Normedcoy military hospital in Tuzla the woman died in Niels' arms.

Friday, 8 April 1994

Today Observation Post Tango 2 of the Swedish 10 Mechcoy, 10 kilometres from the base, sustained a number of hits. Reports mention 'Considerable damage to the kitchen'. Fortunately no casualties. Later I hear that the kitchen was totally destroyed. The UN deals wholesale in euphemisms.

It's as if the grenades are landing closer to the base every day. In the area east of the base new daily records are constantly being broken, 500, 750...

Numbers are innocent; facts recorded dry-eyed.

It had grown imperceptibly busier in the pub. Tijmen hoped there weren't any soldiers among the clientele, and certainly not from his former company. It gave him an uncomfortable feeling when old acquaintances talked to him. He established with relief that he didn't know any of the faces. From an angle above the bar the two old men from the *Muppet Show* looked down at them. Tijmen started greedily on his beer, and wiped the froth from his mouth. His eyes were sparkling.

'The war at Tuzla Airbase and later in the "Thumb" was a forgotten war,' he said, as the waitress brought two new glasses of wheat beer. 'Even then, you lot in the enclave got all the attention, and now, now the enclave has fallen, even more so.'

When they returned from Bosnia there had been an awards ceremony. His sister had come all the way from London for it. Scarcely a word had been said about Alpha Company. The general who spoke had actually mixed up Bravo and Alpha. A hiss had passed through the ranks.

'A forgotten war,' said Tijmen again. He squeezed his eyes half-shut and spoke quietly to himself.

Everywhere soldiers dived for cover. For days the men, wherever they were on the base, had made a mental note of where the shelters were. And yet these kinds of incidents are always unexpected. It's suddenly on top of you. You are waiting for it, but when the moment comes it's still a surprise.

Men who were sleeping after their turn of guard duty sat up in their beds. Sergeant Pos, the company boxing champion, opened his eyes. 'What's happening?' he yelled. Years of training had taught him it was best to follow his intuition. And that intuition told him to wake his buddy as soon as possible. Then, only half awake, he ran down the steps in his underwear, dragging his 'bud' behind him. In the bar tent coffee was dripping from an overturned cup. In the extreme south-east of the base the men of the concertina squad stood stock still in the open fields, as if someone had stopped them with a click of the fingers. Just for a second, then they threw their equipment away and started a long sprint right across the runway.

The whole base was in uproar. Some soldiers were running about in blind panic, others were in good spirits and walked calmly to the nearest cover. They dived deep into their observation posts, helmets and flak jackets were grabbed, swearwords filled the air, binoculars were trained with nervous fingers through peepholes at the hills in the distance, headsets were put on, weapons loaded, orders shouted, heads tucked down between shoulders as if there might be another explosion at any moment. For a second everyone on the base held their breath.

In the command post Herman, the CSM, had dived under the radio table. The command post was the only one not yet reinforced with sandbags.

'My stuff is still in the car,' squeaked Herman.

Speedy charged up the corridor and passed a major who had just arrived at the base. 'This is just incredible, an international airport!' the major yelled after him. He stood there shaking his head. 'It's outrageous,' he kept shouting.

In the distance there was another powerful explosion. Immediately the report came over the company network: '1 x artillery grenade 100 metres beyond the field hospital.'

The doctor reported that everything was OK. The men in the command post followed Speedy's reports from the YPR in which he was touring the base. The Bosnians were reluctant to be shown to the shelters. At the same time Tijmen sent a report to Nordbat.

The officers of Command North-East were jostling about on the stairs that led from the first floor and gathered in the corridor of the headquarters, yelling for information. They crowded around the door of the command post, using their elbows and shoulders to get to the front. An English civilian staff member hurried excitedly to and fro. 'Please don't panic, gentlemen, everything's all right, please don't panic!' The Norwegian major from air-traffic control was sitting hunched in a chair and staring ahead of him without a word. He was pressing his ears tight shut with his fingers. Tijmen posted Corporal IJsselstein by the door so that he could send his reports undisturbed.

'Let only the base commander through,' yelled Tijmen. His voice broke. From the village came the wail of an air-raid siren.

'1 x direct hit on observation post Tango 5, on top of the boiler room.'

Herman called up Tango 5. No answer: the line had been cut. New reports came in of firing. Tijmen closed his eyes and waited for the explosion. A few seconds later there followed a shock of such concentrated explosive power that the windows of the main building rattled.

'1 x artillery grenade 100 metres beyond the command post.'

Then another voice, 'The grenades are being fired from Sugar Hill.'

Tijmen asked Nordbat on the radio for close air support and tanks. And then he informed the battalion in Srebrenica. Half an hour went by. The storm had subsided as quickly as it had blown up. There was not a sound from the radio network. Herman started checking the posts in turn. One by one the soldiers reported themselves present and correct. At Tango 5 he came to a halt.

It was Speedy's voice over the radio: 'Echo here: confirmed, Tango 5 received a direct hit, no casualties.'

Later he told them that the YPR, with four men in it at the time, had missed being hit by a whisker. Only Casterman was in the observation post at the moment of impact. The fragments of the corrugated metal roof had been flung fifteen metres in the air and were hanging in the trees as silent witnesses. When Speedy arrived he found private Casterman sitting wide-eyed at the bottom of the steps.

The bus driver, who had hastily sought cover in the shed next to the boiler room, was still trembling all over, his face contorted in a grimace of astonishment. At the moment of the explosion he had just got out of his vehicle, his hand still on the door. The windscreen had been shattered and the seat had been cut to ribbons by the slivers.

At that moment the first aircraft shot over with a thunderous noise towards Sugar Hill. The pilots looked for the offending guns, their hands poised to release their bombs. But the Serb artillery was silent for the rest of that afternoon.

Tijmen studied the map with the Danish tank commander.

'If those first three rounds had been aimed at the centre of the base, I'd have casualties on my hands now,' said Tijmen.

'Nice of them to warn you first,' the Dane said, puffing eagerly at his pipe, which because of the rain was hanging out of his mouth upside down.

He disappeared into the corridor shouting 'Yippie!' At last he could carry out 'Bøllebank'.

A little later the base was rumbling with Leopard tanks, which were directed to the eastern side of the runway. Their barrels were pointed at Sugar Hill. Operation Bøllebank went very smoothly.

Using the satellite link Tijmen rang the crisis staff in The Hague. An hour later the first journalists rang back for interviews, but by that time Tijmen was already doing the rounds of the base to inspect the craters. Frank spoke to the press. When Tijmen returned he was seething.

Major Frank Platvoet had arrived at the base after all, despite Tijmen's objections. Now, face to face with him, the deputy CO of the battalion was becoming increasingly nervous under his tirade. He said softly, 'Then I'll be off again to battalion staff in Srebrenica.' He seemed as hopeless as when he heard that Cees, who had been a year below him at RMA, had received the news in Srebrenica that he would be promoted to lieutenant-colonel after the mission. Then Frank had assumed a plaintive tone and lamented all the injustice that had been done to him.

With this image in his mind's eye Tijmen suddenly calmed down. He assured Frank that his presence was much appreciated, provided he kept to his own duties. What those duties entailed was completely obscure to everyone, including Frank himself.

Later Tijmen was angry at himself for his own vanity.

How different relations had once been between them. He had been a cadet-ensign when Frank, who at that time he addressed only by his rank, had been commandant to him and the other fourth-year infantry cadets in Harderwijk. Frank always addressed them as 'The Honourable'. Tijmen had never felt less of an Honourable than at that moment. He had experienced the whole of the fourth year as one long prayer, please, to be allowed to succeed.

It was the period when he had learned how to 'get the feel of the terrain'. Terrain relief was referred to as 'gillies', 'gullies' and 'humps'. For years afterwards, Tijmen would view the world through 'infantryman's eyes'. During woodland walks he was capable of sayings like 'a nice mortar position' or when on holiday observing, completely out of the blue, 'This is a good place to fight a rearguard action.'

He remembered that during sports sessions Frank always wanted to join in at football. He would say, 'Watch it, lads, the commandant is taking part.' Frank thought he was a really good footballer. The truth was that no one dared bring him down. Except for David.

It was Frank who had almost had Tijmen expelled from the RMA. He had failed his first practical test for making at least three map-reading errors. David, with whom he shared a room, made sure he was given a second chance. David had also told him he could simply pee in the washbasin; it was a lot better at night than a trip down the cold corridor. David said, 'We're the wbps, the washbasin pee-ers, and everyone's scared of us.'

At his second attempt at map reading he'd just scraped a pass, the only reason he didn't graduate with distinction. Later the governor had set up an investigation into Frank's conduct, but that couldn't make up for the fact that Tijmen had missed this honour.

'I never want to see Frank again,' said Tijmen.

David had got up and grabbed the papers off the table. Tijmen followed him.

On the edge of the terrace there were two seats free. The sunlight had disappeared from the street and a light breeze was cooling Korenmarkt square. Their cigar smoke disappeared into the summer evening warmth in long wisps.

'We didn't hear much about it,' said David when they had sat down. 'Yes, we knew you were under fire at Tuzla Airbase; that was sometimes mentioned at morning briefings. But you must understand we had our own troubles in Srebrenica. Leave sabotaged by the Serbs, cameras that we had to surrender at road-blocks, post that arrived in dribs and drabs, fuel and food not even that.

It was as if Tijmen's eyes forced David to read on.

Sunday, 17 April 1994

Whole nights without proper sleep, fixing and wangling and the constant threat of shelling have really put my nerves to the test.

This afternoon I had a terrible daydream: staring at the image of my own demise. I saw my funeral, my weeping parents, the sad faces of my sisters and the posthumous glory with lots of flowers and consoling words. Killed in action: captain in the red-berets, on a UN mission. The rank, uniform and beret, whether red as in the Netherlands or blue as here, suggest an identity. It was a kind of acute fear of death.

Only on paper can I control reality. Who can I talk to about this uselessness, this futility, human helplessness? To Herman or Speedy? Being horrified and being complicit are not far apart. I feel alone among my own men. It's not who I am, but who they are. It's not who I am but who they *think* I am. The truth is that I'm in total command of my role. *Je est un autre*.

Relations between Herman and Speedy, by the way, are getting worse and worse. They are diametrical opposites: Herman with his gloomy spells and washed-out image, and Speedy with his indomitable energy. Herman is getting more and more annoyed by Speedy's eagerness, his cheerful nature. They write each other curt notes and only speak to each other if there's no alternative. It's time Herman went on leave. Actually I get on pretty well with both of them and so for the last few days have been acting more or less as a go-between.

This morning another two hits on the airbase. One two hundred metres behind the headquarters and another less than a hundred metres from observation post Tango 17. Zevenbergen and Van Bennekom didn't hear it coming. (That means it's really close!)

At the moment when the grenades flew over with a low growling noise I was still in the company's quarters. Fortunately there were again no casualties, though the quartermaster landed with a floating dive on the concrete floor, injuring his arm. Herman welcomed me with no trousers on, his sex hidden by a bundle of clothes. (He was just having a shower.)

Speedy quickly collected me in the YPR, the same procedures as on 14 April. It went without a hitch, but again the jets were too late to carry out a strike.

When I arrived at the site of the impact, the French firefighters' base, fifteen metres from the explosion, turned out to have been riddled with shrapnel. They had taken cover just in time and the French are treasuring the ruined sheets and berets as trophies. They did, though, ask for priority to be given to the strengthening of their building.

The French arrived today to assist the Bosnian fire brigade and so have already had their baptism of fire. A nice welcome. The crater made by the grenade is almost two metres across; a 155 millimetre calibre, we concluded.

It's striking that the Serbs are leaving the runway untouched. They are probably planning to use it themselves in the future.

Monday, 18 April 1994

The command post has finally been secured with sandbags and so-called 'defence walls'. For the time being we no longer have to dive under the radio table during shelling.
 Every day it gets busier on the airbase. There are now Irish and Finnish engineers, Norwegian air-traffic controllers, Russian policemen, Dutch military police, French and Bosnian fire fighters and a French mine-clearance team. The three Russians moved to Tuzla last night because it has become 'too dangerous' on the base.
 This evening I read some of *Hotel Atonaal* by Hans Keller, which I carry around with me all day. It's the first time since I arrived that the words are really getting through to me, as if up to now I have been dyslexic. It's a lack of concentration I think. I need privacy to read properly. It's only now that there are gaps in the schedule. The book is about the experimental poets of the 1950s. Keller writes: 'A girl called Rita, who during the day had hockey knees and in the evenings a summer dress, lodged with her aunt in an imposing house overlooking Kenau Park. That became Russian Lady Park. I kept it secret from Harry, because we were both in love with the same mystery'.

  'How charming the Russian lady is
  And listen to what she says'

These lines are by Hans Lodeizen. They remind me of the girl in Srebrenica.

Friday, 22 April 1994

This morning six grenades and again no casualties. We're almost getting used to them.
 At the moment of the first hit I'm outside smoking a cigar. Everyone starts running; I don't want to give in to my fear and try to walk as calmly as possible to the command post. Outwardly

I appear unmoved but when I get to the main building and take my pulse, I count a hundred and eighty beats.

The grenades were fired just as an aircraft had landed. The Jordanian radar unit, who were being brought in on the plane, were assembling at the moment the shelling started. Half of them ran for the shelters, the others got back on board. The aircraft returned immediately to Split. Next to the runway lie half-opened suitcases and bags left behind by the Jordanians.

Total of mines found to date: 58. (Still about two years to go.) The French clearance team have set up an exhibition of disabled mines on a table at the entrance to the main building, in which there is a lot of interest.

Herman is in Split with the second leave group, and phones. They have heard the news about the shelling and are worried.

This afternoon I met the Jordanian commander, a man of Mediterranean appearance and a mask-like face, and had a strange conversation with him. The man spoke appalling English and to add force to his words kept pinching me hard in my forearm. To my comment that the base was in good shape and that unlike Srebrenica there was even 'fuel', 'sandbags' and 'mail', he replied, 'I don't think they will allow us male.'

'No mail?' I asked.

'Yes, male,' said the Jordanian, increasing the pressure on my arm. 'You know, as in female.'

Wednesday, 27 April 1994

Since the last shelling no other planes have landed. Final go-ahead for the mission in the Sapna Thumb. On 1 June we will take over the duties of the Swedes.

Thursday, 5 May 1994

The men of the kitchen group have secretly had a blue-and-yellow name tag made at Nordbat with *King of Tuzla* on it in black letters. I wore it all day.

David leafed through the papers. He was more talkative than usual.

Was this the same David, the unbreakable David? His words made Tijmen uncertain. It was as if David's energy had ebbed away over the years. How long ago was it that they had both been elected to the Senate of the Cadet Corps? He had of course immediately agreed, but David had first politely refused the post, not once but twice.

For the first time David talked about his condition, with carefully chosen words. The discomfort in the summer he had learned to live with, and the ointment he applied every day was 'a miracle cure'. Tijmen had always felt that the condition was in some way connected to David's outward equilibrium. As if his body were compensating. He had never dared tell him this, fearing it might lead to an estrangement.

David had never had the ambition to be a general, and always had to laugh when Tijmen mentioned it. He smoked the occasional cigar, but never more than two, and drank in moderation. David who seemed to have everything under control, was closer than ever.

Monday, 9 May 1994

The reconnaissance patrol has just returned from observation post Tango 2, which we will take over from the Swedes on 1 June. Speedy and Joris act tough and say that they've joined the club of those who've been shot at, but their eyes tell a different story.

'We were in the last vehicle, behind the Swedes,' says Speedy. 'We had observed the firing from Sugar Hill and suddenly the patrol came to a halt in the middle of Rainci Gornji. Joris and I immediately went to take a look. The Swedes wanted to continue but the road was blocked by a woman's body, burned black, lying right next to where the grenade had struck. To the right and left people were running into the verge. Nothing more to be done. A little distance away lay a man. In order to reach him we had to wade through his intestines. Blood was gushing from his belly. And the weird thing is it didn't smell of anything.'

Joris says nothing.

'Next to the man lay a bike. A small right shoe stood on the asphalt. Remnants of flesh were sticking out of it. To the right of the road half a girl's torso was hanging in the branches of a tree. So her body must have been hurled about five or six metres. A length of small intestine of about a metre was hanging out. I was furious.'

Joris nods. Speedy speaks even faster than normal.

'And those Swedes wanted to go on,' says Speedy indignantly. Again, 'They fucking well wanted to go on.'

On the way to Tango 2 they had tried to work off their anger, but as Speedy tells his story he gets angry again. 'On the way back we saw people putting the last body into a van. And now every time I hear a strike I think of that family.'

I order the men to see the psychologist for a debriefing.

David looked up.

'We came under fire in Srebrenica too,' he said sharply. 'Our patrols especially were regularly fired on.'

For a moment this meeting threatened to take a different turn: as if they were competing to see who had been shot at most. Then Tijmen started talking. Soon he was totally absorbed in his own story.

Still half an hour to kill before he was due to go to the command post. On the frame of the open window there were more and more flies. He started killing them, squashing them. He laid into them. Wham, two at once! Not bad for a first attempt. Would it help if he lit a cigar? He reached for the tin and fished one out. He was starting to run through his supply at a great rate. Tomorrow he should write home. He calculated to himself: five days there, five days back; that makes ten days, a tin a day. Enough, he worked out with satisfaction and lit the thin cigar.

The new quarters which he had moved into after the staff of UNPROFOR North-East Command had requisitioned the company building had thick walls, so it stayed pleasantly cool all day long inside.

The noises wafting from the village just outside the fence penetrated the room. In the distance there was the pinched bark of a dog. The base was swarming with feral cats and stray dogs. Odd that the animals always dared to come back; only yesterday the military police had shot three. It was as if the creatures knew that they were safe in the minefields that were all around the base. And shooting them with a Fal – a rifle with a guaranteed range of three hundred metres – was completely pointless. You shot right through them. And then, as had happened yesterday, you were stuck with a dog in the minefield, howling at a pitch that made you wince.

Music was coming very softly from Speedy's room. 'A decrepit house,' sang the drawling voice of Johnny Jordaan, a one-time popular singer. Soon Speedy was going to buy mini-Nikes for his two-year-old son.

What had Speedy said about the bodies in Rainci Gornji? 'There was no smell.' Tijmen had never seen a dead person at close quarters himself. He had, though, followed with his binoculars the mortar shelling to which the people in the fields to the east of the village were regularly subjected, but that was unreal. From a great distance he had seen them fleeing, right across the minefields, as if they were dancing barefoot on a cold tiled floor.

It was a quarter to twelve. Tijmen put on the belt with his pistol on it and grabbed the helmet and flak jacket from the corner.

Outside there was a moment of glorious silence, an intoxicating evening smelling of blossom. The evening air seemed to refresh him a little. It was pitch black, but Tijmen knew the road like the palm of his hand. If he followed the asphalt, the gentle bend to the right, in a few hundred metres he would come to the crossing, then cut across and soon be lit by the lights of the main building.

He no longer even heard the noise of firing and impact. In the distance, the weak glow from the windows of the main building cast shadows on the surface of the road.

There was no sign of anyone in the corridor of the staff building. There was not even the slightest sound from the first floor, where Command North-East was located. He was reminded of the Dutch staff colonel who had said to him, 'Now, if you lose a bit of weight, you'll go far.'

Raymond called out vaguely in greeting.

'I'm staying another half hour or so,' he said and then, 'You can read a bit longer.'

The corporal next to him, Daniel, was sleeping with his head on his hands, snoring loudly. Tijmen sat down at the table, got out his Discman and put the headphones in his ears. Through the music he could hear Raymond checking on observation posts via the radio.

'No details, about fifty firings in the last hour,' he called out above the music.

Tijmen nodded and opened his book, but didn't read. Raymond, his clerk; because of a lack of personnel he took his turn at the radio with the other NCOs. Raymond, with his stillborn child.

The door was flung open. Poortman, the Dutch major from North-East Command, came in. He went to the table and pretended to thump the Discman. Tijmen hated his jovial manner. Raymond didn't hesitate for a moment, but leapt up and pounced on the major with his full hundred kilos. His feet lost their grip and the struggle continued on the ground, where Raymond soon had the major in an arm lock. Tijmen still pretended to be reading.

Someone knocked the hat stand over with his feet, and it fell to the floor with a deafening crash.

Shortly afterward the two men stood grinning at each other with some embarrassment, dusting themselves off. A bit odd really, a sergeant jumping a major. Inwardly Tijmen was smiling.

Poortman left without saying good night. Tijmen got up, slapped Raymond on the shoulder and said, 'It's Alpha against the rest of the world.'

Daniel had taken over from Raymond, who had disappeared to the living quarters. After he had given the corporal instructions to wake him if anything, however trivial, came up, he went to the room further down the corridor where he slept when he was on duty. One night in three: the other turns were taken by Herman and Speedy. And now Herman was on leave, every other night.

He took off his T-shirt, got the shaving mirror and held it at arm's length. Then he took his loins between his thumb and forefinger and surveyed the effect. Everyone around him seemed to be worried about the beginnings of corpulence.

Ha ha, all the local commanders here were fat.

He put the mirror away and sat down on the bed. He tried to think of nothing for a moment, but after ten minutes got up and paced about the room. 'It was in the summer of '92,' he said under his breath.

A confusing restlessness. He, Tijmen, had been up for everything, parachute jumping, abseiling from rock faces, anything at all. 'A grand and compelling life' – the words of the poet had raced through his head. Once he'd passed Utrecht the restlessness increased further. He was an outcast.

The neon lights of the Mercure Hotel could be seen from afar. They came closer and closer. He didn't even bother to drive into town.

In the room he dialled the number with trembling fingers. The phone rang twice. Then a voice, 'This is Denise van Amstel from Amstel Call Girls.'

In a reedy little boy's voice he replied, 'This is Rob.'

'Where are you, Rob?' she said with a touch of sarcasm in her voice. 'Then I can call you back.'

He gave her the name of the hotel and the room number.

The telephone rang. He hesitated but finally answered.

Denise asked about his requirements, 'White or coloured?'
He said it made no difference. Then she mentioned the price. He counted the banknotes. 'One hour.'
'How did you hear about us?'
His voice faltered.
'We always ask.'
'An article in the paper,' he answered, for the first time truthfully.
Finally she asked his age, as it was 'nice to know' for the girl.
Twenty minutes later he was rung again, she had arrived. She would take 'five minutes or so' to get up to his room. He listened with his ear to the door. There were men's voices in the hall. Was reception in the know? The five minutes extended to ten.

The door opened and the smell of eau de cologne wafted in: his grandmother's fragrance. In front of him was a redhead in a blue dress that fitted tightly round her thighs, with round breasts, red evening shoes with stiletto heels, and a short fur coat. There was a ladder in her black nylons just below her right knee.
She flopped into a chair and threw her enormous handbag on the table. She wanted a drink first. He wasn't prepared for that, though he was for the fact 'that he must pay first'.
While the girl carefully folded the three hundred-guilder notes, she said firmly, 'The minibar is in the cupboard opposite the shower.'
She had a diet coke and he had a beer. He sipped cautiously and tried to suppress the burps that kept coming up. She put her card next to the ashtray: it had a red heart on it.
'I have to make a call,' she said.
He heard her voice from afar, 'Yes, not bad... One hour.'
She nestled back in her chair.
Hoarsely he stammered, 'Can I sit on your lap for a moment?'
He kissed her gently on the lips. She didn't kiss back. Close up she didn't smell of perfume, she smelled of chewing gum. His hands groped for her breasts. With a deft movement she slid

the straps off her narrow shoulders. They spilled out together, a perfect handful. Not shapeless and flabby, but firm and round. She put his glasses on the table.

'You've got cold hands,' she said, pushing him away. 'Come on, let's lie down.'

With a squeal she threw herself back on the bed. He quickly took off his clothes and crawled towards her on his belly. Her clothes were scattered over the sheets in small heaps. She lay there passively, with eyes closed. He tried to think of the socks that were still on his feet.

'What do you like doing best?'

'Stroking.'

'I don't like them,' said the girl, pushing her breasts up with her hands.

She spread her legs and ran her fingers down across her belly. Before he was able to touch her, he came.

'Doesn't matter.'

She reached for her handbag.

'Have you got a light?'

A hotel room on the edge of Amsterdam, through the window the lights of the city twinkled. He, Tijmen, still a twenty-nine-year-old virgin – star sign Libra – smoked his very first joint. The wet patch in the sheet stuck to his buttocks.

They talked trivia for a quarter of an hour: about the nice room and her studies. Suddenly she said, 'You're very romantic, aren't you?'

'Quite.'

'I don't like romantic men.'

'I can be pretty hard too.'

'Are you going into Amsterdam tonight?' asked the girl.

He didn't reply, but crept close to her and hugged her tight. She reached for his wildly throbbing sex.

'Can you come again?'

He stroked her skin with the tips of his fingers. Low down on her belly there was a red tuft.

'Oh, go on, go on, on that little button... a bit differently each time.'

'She groaned orgiastically, like a dying animal and stroked the inside of his thighs. A sudden sensation made him catch his breath, and a moment later his sperm was dripping over her fingers. She jumped up abruptly.

'I'm going to freshen up,' she called over her shoulder.

He grabbed his glasses off the coffee table and was just in time to see her full buttocks disappear into the shower. From the bathroom came the sound of splashing water.

Before she left she asked, 'Or would you like another hour?'

By the door she said in a suddenly broad Amsterdam accent, 'Bye then, darling. Are you sure?'

A fleeting kiss on his cheek.

He looked at the radio alarm: that was forty-five minutes.

The next morning on the motorway he felt in his pocket and threw the visiting card furiously onto the dashboard. On the gentle turn-off to Utrecht he had a slight urge to drive straight on. Screeching brakes, the car skidded. For a second he felt something like a death wish. Just in time he straightened the car. In a determined movement he grabbed the card and threw it out of the window. It blew away under the guard rail and with it her name.

He had simply driven home as if nothing had happened. With a furious gesture Tijmen unscrewed the top of the expensive black pen his parents had given him before he left. He wrote a few words in his diary and stopped. He was alive and hadn't died, certainly not as a virgin. He lay down on the bed, stretched out and fell into a deep sleep.

He immediately recognised Heather's slim figure, still not a day over fifteen. But however loud he shouted she didn't recognise him and walked straight past. A little later she got on the train. He ran to the doors. Too late. His arm got caught. His own eyes were mirrored in her child's eyes.

He woke sweating at a quarter to eight, checked quickly with Daniel to ask for any last-minute details and hurried, unshaven and sleepy, to the morning meeting which began at eight o'clock on the dot. He fought back a surge of nausea.

In his hand he was clutching an attaché case. He remembered the general who had said, 'A soldier with an attaché case isn't a soldier.' Just as the military winter and summer had been abolished – the fixed times when sleeves went up and down were the general's hobby-horse – the attaché cases had gained ground. Now it was more like: an officer without an attaché case isn't an officer.

It was the grist of images from the past, the roaring mechanism of his imagination. He tried to concentrate on the voice of the Norwegian colonel who was chairing the meeting.

His thoughts wandered off to his schooldays. In the year he met Heather, he had become ill, his marks had slumped dramatically and he had had to repeat a year. The vague ailments which the doctor called 'psychosomatic' had steadily worsened. He had found himself in her class, for three years, until the final exams.

While the Norwegian major from air-traffic control repeated for the umpteenth time in his shrill voice that no one should go anywhere near the runway or the control tower without his express permission, shreds of memory came into Tijmen's mind like phantoms.

In the class photo he was sitting very close to her; one person in between them, her girlfriend. Heather and he were both gazing the other way. The rest were looking at the camera.

Furious looks from her girlfriends who cycled after him and teased him as he rode home from school. Just before he turned off, the hurtful remarks behind his back. The whispered conversations that stopped when he approached.

Her elder sister, whom he happened to meet at a party, who pushed herself up against him during the dancing and hissed, 'You'd like to, but you can't, can you...?'

He had never told anyone about these things. There had been a reunion of his final-year class in 1987, a year after the RMA. Heather kissed him when they met. She sat close to him. He was still just as shy. They didn't talk privately, though they did listen to each other's conversations with others. Several times he saw her asking a classmate what he had been talking about. When he said goodbye he knew for sure he would never see her again.

Yet he had bumped into her on three occasions since. She had moved to Arnhem. And on none of those occasions had he dared speak to her.

The high-pitched voice of the Russian policeman. One more and it would be his turn. The Russian, a fat chap with a sardonic smile, was puffing with the heat. He was so fat that his neck seemed to be missing. He had piercing eyes behind his steamed-up lenses in thick silver frames. On his upper lip there was a large brownish-black wart with two long hairs sticking out. When he opened his mouth he revealed a row of brown teeth. The Russian had served his time as commandant of military police in the Black Sea port of Sebastopol. With the base commander his behaviour was almost servile, but still, or perhaps for that very reason, you could easily imagine him as a cruel interrogator.

Now the Norwegian colonel addressed Tijmen. He heard his own clipped voice reporting the previous day's events in Rainci Gornji.

Tijmen lit up a new cigar. David's face gave little away.

'At night the sounds were different from during the day,' said Tijmen, 'and there were mosquitoes and horseflies. The infestation came mostly from the unusable toilet across the corridor. At night I sometimes pissed through the hole in the floor. The night was the reverse side of the day, with distorting shadows on the walls. I did my last round of the observation posts late in the evening, when the base was guarded by sixteen soldiers at most, and intruders crept in to steal diesel from the power generating units.'

Tijmen took a deep breath. David drew a sharp distinction between work and private life. Perhaps that was the greatest difference between them. He had once told David that he saw being an officer as his vocation. David had grinned and shook his head. For a long time he had wanted to be like David.

'The night was always the time for thinking, alone, naked, stifling memories in the pillow. During the day I went through the motions, spent hours in the meeting room. I was seldom alone; there was always someone who needed me urgently. At night I was no one, I woke up every hour from a light sleep. Sweating, getting my bearings from the glow that came in through the window. But when the dawn rose above the hills, the King of Tuzla awoke.'

It was seven o'clock. Tijmen got up and stretched. He hummed and fished his sports shorts from the chair. The sun was shining. There was Milan walking along. He must be going for coffee in the bar. Milan, the Serb interpreter, who told him how he had heard in the Balkan Grill, his local, how you could get out of military service by becoming an interpreter for the UN. His father was one of the leaders of the Serb community in Tuzla. Now, after two years of war, there were still five thousand Serbs living in the town. Milan had told him that his father was on the board of the Orthodox Church in the centre. Tijmen passed it regularly when he went for meetings at Nordbat. The church with its yellowy white plasterwork, outwardly intact, still dominated the park on the edge of the old town.

A few lads from the field kitchen were playing football on the field between the living quarters. There was only a small area of it left: the Jordanians had pitched their tents there on the patch that had only been cleared of mines since the Queen's Birthday. On the Queen's Birthday Alpha Company's team had beaten the French 6-3. Joris was running leaps around the field. After each leap he glanced at his watch. Not until the third leap did he see Tijmen standing at the window. He waved briefly then looked at his watch again. The Jordanians watched him pass in amazement.

Tijmen didn't even want to think about the Jordanians. They had cost him his plastic toilet seats, because they refused to sit. They even shat in his showers, or so the Swedes maintained. The base commander said that *they*, not the Jordanians must be careful. He said, 'Before you know it we'll be accused of discrimination.' But when on the Queen's Birthday the Jordanians had fired a machine gun in the air to add lustre to the festivities, even he had been furious.

Tijmen hung a towel round his neck, picked up his toilet bag and stepped into his bath slippers. A walkie-talkie dangled from his right shoulder. Only when he got outside did he realise how oppressively warm it was. In the shower room Sluiter told him that letters had arrived and, at last, newspapers. Every day followed the same well-worn pattern, but it was as if on days when there was mail the whole camp was a little more cheerful. Even the report on his walkie-talkie that Tuzla was under heavy Serb artillery fire did little to change that. The shelling might be in revenge for yesterday's shelling of Brčko by the Bosnians. The hospital had been hit by three grenades and there had been three casualties. All UN traffic had been restricted until further notice.

'The second platoon particularly has had a lot of post,' said Sluiter.

Some soldiers had photos from as many as four different women. Just before they were sent out Sergeant Pos's group had been featured in a national newspaper, *De Telegraaf*, in full combat gear. There were flowery greetings cards with inscriptions like: 'Good luck, a Granny'. But there was also a man who had sent a photo of his wife and a big Alsatian dog. He had written: 'I'm looking for a big tough military man for them'.

Frank emerged from the shower. The hubbub at the wash basins stopped abruptly. The deputy battalion commander wasn't very popular with the men. Tijmen didn't look at him, quickly brushed his teeth and splashed some water over his face. That week he and Frank had visited the Muslim divisional commander who was responsible for the whole of the Sapna Thumb, in preparation for his new task. The general was based in a white villa hidden in a wood near Rainci Gornji. Frank had taken off his boots at the door, even before anyone had spoken to him.

He had treated the Muslim commander with grovelling servility, and wouldn't stop talking about 'showing the flag'. He nodded in agreement at the Muslims' every word. Later he had said, 'Giving way is often the best policy.'

Frank said so many differing things that Tijmen didn't even know what he really thought. It was part of his armour, as if he wanted to avoid every cliff that might damage his career: a model of helpfulness. The more Tijmen stood up to Frank, the more Frank retreated into his shell. During the conversation he realised that this was a potentially lethal combination: a frightened rabbit with the need to assert himself. Frank's whole behaviour was a cry for acknowledgement from his wife, from his superiors and now also from the commanders of the warring parties. On the way back to the base Tijmen had tried to flatter Frank by saying that on their new mission – 'you're a major, after all' – he would have to maintain contacts with North-East Command, which he was doing anyway, and with Muslim officials, 'from divisional level upwards'.

The faint, scarcely perceptible shadow came closer. Tijmen cleared his throat and spat the phlegm out on the ground. He straightened his back. His heart was pounding high in his chest. Just before the living quarters he turned round suddenly and looked straight into Frank's grinning face. In his hand he had two cigars, one of which he gave to Tijmen. They went in together. Tijmen had scarcely ever seen him so excited; usually Frank did not get beyond verbal formalities.

Tijmen smiled his friendliest smile. When he complimented Frank on finding a new location for the company in Simin Han, Frank beamed like a little child. Yet Tijmen knew that Frank wouldn't hesitate to stab him in the back; that he was waiting for Tijmen to slip up. If there was even a single casualty he would be bound to say, 'You see, I told you so.' He knew and Frank knew he knew. That was his only protection.

'I'll smoke it later,' said Tijmen, 'after the morning meeting,' and disappeared into his room.

He shut the door behind him, clenching his fist round the cigar, which crumbled to dust in his hand.

David went inside to pay the bill. Tijmen had never told him so much before. When he came back Tijmen said, 'The story isn't finished.'
David muttered his excuses and poked him in the ribs.
'You know, Tijmen, you'll get there.'
Did he detect pity in the look David gave him?
'We can just arrange to meet another time, can't we?' said David.
It sounded like a final farewell.
They walked across the street together to the taxi rank, still together.

The light was already out in the private house on the corner. The train on the embankment bored its way through the night, and the leaves rustled in the trees.
David was his danger zone, because he would tell him everything and David would not keep silent. Not David. And suddenly Tijmen hoped David would tell everyone.

PART V
AN EVENING IN SIMIN HAN

Tijmen clenched his fists. 'I'm not ducking anything anymore,' he said softly. He opened the door to the corridor and climbed the stairs slowly, bringing his breathing under control. In the harsh neon light he was seized by a feeling that time had stood still. Once he could easily have bought a house, saved for the future, but he had always stayed in the same flat. In the meantime almost all the residents had moved, except for him.

Inside he slumped into a chair. The meeting with David had set something in motion that couldn't be undone. As if in a whirlpool, he was sucked back by the past to the reconnaissance patrol he had been on to the 'Sapna Thumb' in mid-May 1994. His surroundings became blurred, as if he were back in the area where Alpha Company was to carry out its duties that summer.

Tijmen grabbed the handle and lowered his commander's chair with a clatter. Milan, with his head cocked to one side, was huddled on the back seat – Milan, who before they left had asked timidly if it was sensible to take him along, as a Serb, into the 'Thumb'. But he couldn't afford to think of Milan any longer. He had to concentrate on the road ahead of him, so that later he could remember the route exactly.

The main road led further and further into the area. 'It takes more than six hours to drive from the compound to the north of the Sapna Thumb,' Larsson had said. Tijmen's YPR was the second armoured vehicle behind the Swedish commander, who was in command of the patrol.

'Main road' was perhaps too grand a title for the path that regularly turned into a cart-track. They drove down heavily shaded lanes, where the foliage brushed the helmets of the on-board gunners', along deep ravines and narrow winding donkey paths, the vehicles regularly having to roll back a bit and negotiate obstacles in order to keep going. People at the roadside waved at the armoured patrol.

At last Tijmen was in the area where he wanted to be, a kind of excrescence from the Bosnian federation, reaching like a bent thumb deep into Bosnian Serbia. Still the Serbs had not succeeded in conquering the area. Here Bosnian Serbia, apart from the corridor at Brčko, was at its narrowest. In clear weather from the hills above Sapna you could see the power station at Loznica, tens of kilometres away. The Thumb represented a direct threat to all Serb traffic to and from the north.

In Sapna the convoy stopped opposite the emergency hospital. An ambulance with panting siren raced away from the site. The people of the village crowded round the vehicle. A few children were playing with a home-made ball. One of them stuck up his thumb, 'Van Basten, number one!' Larsson decided to visit the commander of the 205th Muslim brigade, but his headquarters were deserted. After some insistence a sentry told them that he was at a forward position near Goduš.

For half an hour the patrol drove down a semi-hardened path that wound along the mountainside. Sometimes there was a glimpse of the threatening transmission mast of Stolice, at a height of over nine hundred metres, from which the Serbs could survey the whole area around Sapna. The Serbs, whose motto was: 'Victory begins at Stolice'. It was as if the exploding grenades could smell the tracks of the vehicles.

Just before Goduš Patrick yelled down the intercom, 'Christ, bodies!'

Seven zipped-up body bags lay in the verge. Through the thin material the shapes of human remains were just visible. Further on the road was packed with furious Muslim fighters who were reluctant to make way for them.

The convoy of armoured vehicles stopped at the white house where the Muslim commander was staying. He was waiting outside. He was unshaven, his eyes were bulging and bloodshot, and his whole body was shivering.

Along the walls of the small room where Larsson and Tijmen were received sat silent Muslim fighters with their weapons between their knees; dark men, some staring straight ahead with empty eyes, others playing cards. No one made any effort to disguise the tension. The room had been transformed into a command post. Two soldiers came in and out with boxes of ammunition. Someone was rolling out a spool of wire.

The Muslim commander was sitting in the middle of the room on a chair. Larsson and Tijmen and their interpreter sat opposite him on a two-seat sofa. Tijmen could feel the heat of Milan's sweaty body. The commander had only just begun talking when the telephone rang. He answered, putting a hand over his left ear. All eyes were on him.

'Are you sure?' translated Milan softly.

The Muslim commander listened for a while and then slammed the receiver down. He suddenly started moving. He was trembling and his hands were trembling along with him. He quickly unfolded the map in front of him and signalled energetically that Larsson and Tijmen must leave the room. New fighting had erupted. Milan just had time to say, 'He apologises.'

Outside, his men, weapons held aloft, were yelling. Their cries of: 'Allah! Akbar Allah! Allah! Akbar!' rang through the valley.

The vehicles crawled over the ridge, which was in direct view of the Bosnian Serb mortars. From one instant to the next the landscape changed character. The nail of the Thumb was less mountainous, and also more fertile. But it offered less protection to its inhabitants than the mountains they had seen earlier. They passed a hamlet with the remains of houses that had been shot to pieces: draughty carcasses with their cellars open to the sky. On the way they met a few soldiers. There was also a woman among them, the words 'Allah-u-Akbar' sewn onto her uniform. As happened everywhere, she asked, 'Is the road through Kalesija secure?'

Tijmen screwed up his eyes. Abundant sunlight flooded the rolling landscape. The fields stretched out in front of him, deep, deep green. It looked unusually beautiful. Once there must have been livestock grazing here, but now there wasn't an animal to be seen. A panoramic view of the reservoir down below, shimmering ultramarine and green in the bright light; on its southern side a small church with a large cross on the roof, surrounded by water, like a holiday snap. The vehicles slowly descended the steep hill, tacking carefully so as not to slip off the path.

On the asphalted road in Brzava all hell was suddenly let loose. The grenades landed so close that the blast shook the armoured vehicles to and fro. Patrick panicked. He started yelling, 'Why don't those Swedes drive on?'

The YPR was wedged between the Swedish vehicles in a spot where the road was a little lower. To the left and right the embankment towered above the on-board weapons. Tijmen pushed his right calf against the engine panel. The reassuring vibration of the diesel engine ran up his thigh. If the Serbs wanted to hit him, they would have to aim very well. Later Tijmen realised that they could have done that easily: for two years the Serbs had held daily practice sessions at shooting right in the 'jackpot', as they called it in mortar training at Harderwijk.

They couldn't do anything about it: it was impossible for Danish tanks to penetrate the Thumb, and air support always arrived too late anyway. Tijmen started sweating. Putting someone behind the on-board weapon – a 50 calibre machine gun without any protection – was pure suicide. All you could do was get the hell out, like frightened rabbits.

Tijmen's life now depended on the competence of the Serbs and Larsson's skill at dodging their grenades, but mostly on chance. Never before had he been so close to death. It felt good.

Finally the Swedish commander decided to risk it. The vehicles followed one by one, accelerating like athletes from the starting blocks, enveloped in a cloud of dust that was driven higher by each successive vehicle and settled only minutes later. Scores of anxious eyes kept a close watch through periscopes on the hostile bank of the lake. Over the radio came the harassed voice of Larsson, shouting that they must take the correct turn-off. Engines screaming, the vehicles climbed the slope.

They tore into Teočak at high speed. Precisely at that moment four bodies were being taken for burial at once, swaddled in rags. Behind them walked just three people. Only a year ago the whole village would have turned up. Now the people watched silently from the shade of their houses as the small group passed, battered into submission by the daily shelling.

Only here in Teočak did Tijmen realise that his new area was three times as large as the enclave of Srebrenica, with between twenty and forty thousand citizens and no fewer than three Muslim brigades. Over against them was the Serbs' heavy weaponry, while he had three times fewer troops at his disposal than Verbeek in Srebrenica.

It was still spring, but nature here was at least two months ahead of the Netherlands. Winter had gone from the air, and the wind became sultrier by the day. 'And the fighting is getting heavier,' said the people in the village.

They were received in the local town hall where in a corner stood a large Bosnian flag: six fleur-de-lis on a blue background with a white bar through it. The windows were taped with thick plastic from UNHCR, so that the faces of those they were talking to became blurred, like ghosts. They were given large glasses of orange squash to cool them off. The chair of the municipal council gave a long speech in the rhetorical style so customary here. Communism was far from dead.

While they were exposed to the searching looks of their hosts, Tijmen looked only at the polluted water from which the orange squash had been made. (He had been inoculated in the Netherlands against diphtheria, tetanus, polio and typhus.) The squash tasted of sand.

After the reception they quickly unloaded the food parcels and medicine. The rumble of mortar and artillery fire sounded dangerously close.

The local GP, whose work consisted mainly of treating gunshot wounds and amputating limbs, was delighted with their medicine. His practice was a gruesome world of blood-soaked sheets, decay and decomposition, combined with the pungent smell of chloroform and Lysol, and outside the pale faces of inquisitive children in the spring sunshine. Teočak's doctor was a dark, long-haired figure with the jaded appearance of someone who has looked death in the face too many times. In response to the question as to how on earth he performed operations amid these ruins he made the sound of an imaginary saw.

Hasim Omanović went into the room where the sick and wounded lay, the room with the blacked-out windows. He grabbed a bottle from the cupboard, poured the rakija into a glass and emptied it in one gulp. Rakija was the anaesthetic for himself and his patients. Right at the back were the beds of two men who had come stumbling in yesterday. The younger grabbed him by the arm every time he passed. The elder was too weak for that. He didn't even have the strength to bring a spoon to his mouth. When he tried he got halfway up his ribcage. Breathlessly he asked the boy to feed him. Hasim had forgotten their names. He wanted to forget them.

He kept away from them as far as possible. He had patients to look after: wounded people whose lungs were in danger of haemorrhaging or who were the parchment-yellow colour of hepatitis, and men with complicated fractures or filthy, brownish yellow wounds in which the maggots were having a field day.

What could Hasim do when the younger man told him about the camp near Bijeljina? The camps everyone had heard of but no one knew. All he could do was patch up the weakened men, build up their strength so that they could walk to Tuzla. For months they had lived on one bowl of thin cabbage soup a day and the occasional hunk of bread; they wore the same clothes without once being able to wash.

They had told him about the drunken guards who came into the gym in the evenings and beat them with truncheons; the guards who called themselves 'superčetniks'. The younger had told the story. Each time he said something, the elder gestured with his thin, powerless hands as if he were trying to say, 'Exactly, that's right.'

The young man had told Hasim how the men almost crushed each other to death in order to escape the blows, 'As if they were trying to hit us right through the walls.' Sometimes he laughed as he told the story. It wasn't a human laugh. He described how the bigger guys had stood on the outside to protect them. How some couldn't stand it any longer and charged the guards, heading for certain death. How occasionally someone was taken away for interrogation, and the way they looked when they came back. How they slept in their own faeces while all night long loud music blared through the hall. How strong young men died of diphtheria. And how they themselves had to paint slogans on the wall: 'Muslims to Turkey'. About the cruel games that were played: squat jumps they had been forced to make for hours on end until the blood vessels in their ears seemed to snap, till they went almost crazy with the buzzing in their ears. And about men who were raped with the barrel of a rifle, and sons who had to satisfy their own fathers.

No one could expect him, Hasim, to play psychiatrist. When first he had arrived in the village he would get worked up about this sort of thing, but gradually his emotions had become anaesthetised and he just did his work routinely. He had long ago lost his sense of date and time.

He was by himself. The girl who helped him had received no training at all. The aid organisations had not visited the village since December. There was only one access road. They were caught like rats in a Serb trap: the 'Četniks' had already surrounded the village on three sides.

To the south the doctors were still being relieved. In the practice in Rainci Gornji, in the emergency hospital in Sapna, the hand of Tuzla was still felt and the doctors were on a rota. But no one wanted to be here in Teočak.

The only thing he could do was to load the badly wounded on a farm cart under cover of darkness and take them to the bridge on the south side of the lake, to the bridge that had been on the point of collapse for weeks. Then the ambulance would come from Sapna to transfer the wounded, at least if the telephone worked.

He put on a new white coat, covered in rusty brown stains. He had boiled it yesterday, but it hadn't helped much. Again he poured some rakija into a glass and went round the beds. He gave the men who were still awake a few small sips. Their faces seemed to take on a beatific expression when he gave them a drink. He went back to the washbasin, rinsed the glass with water and chlorine and sat down at his desk.

From outside came the slowly retreating sound of armoured vehicles. But he didn't hear it any more. Hasim Omanović had fallen asleep with his head on his desk.

Stari Teočak was stuck to the side of a mountain, its houses huddled together. Although this village too was in full view of the Serbs, it was scarcely damaged. Tijmen and Larsson walked down the middle of the street, with two soldiers ahead and behind who kept taking up new positions, and sent messages back to the command vehicle on a walkie-talkie.

It was almost two o'clock, but nothing moved, Stari Teočak was silent and so empty it seemed abandoned, and yet Tijmen constantly felt he was being observed by invisible eyes. They walked right round the village, up and down, past terraces, through streets to yet more streets, past wooden houses and houses with white plasterwork. Not one was identical to the next. The village purred peacefully in the spring afternoon. Still they stayed as far as possible in the deep shadow cast by the houses, out of sight of the Serbs, looking to the left, to the right, more and more on edge. Just when Tijmen thought that they would go on and on walking, Larsson stopped by a house.

As they entered it smelled of thyme, and weeds grew rampant between the slabs on the terrace. For the first time since the outbreak of war the occupants could drink coffee outside again.

More chairs were pulled up, pleasantries exchanged. The two soldiers who had come with them had taken up position flat on their stomachs next to the front door, scanning the area with their binoculars. Obviously the UN presence on the eastern side of the Thumb was a deterrent to the Bosnian Serbs.

Rakija appeared on the table, dried prunes and baklava, and when they attempted to take off their boots out of politeness the family shook their heads vehemently. Larsson spoke admiringly of the view they had. The head of the family, still quite young and vital, spoke of peace, but only when that house over there… He stared doggedly into the distance.

That night they stayed over in Teočak with the Swedes. From five to ten Tijmen occupied an observation post north of the village with his armoured vehicle. People from the surrounding area brought prunes and dark-red cherries, as if they were liberators. His men were invited in turn for tea in the nearest house. In those five hours, two hundred and fifty mortar shells fell between his vehicle and the front line three kilometres away. Tijmen realised that if three shells landed next to Tuzla Hotel, where the international press was based, the world would be deeply shocked.

A momentary sense of relaxation was felt late in the evening, with Swedish songs and stories of home. Then they went to bed, in a house abandoned by the occupants and offered by the town council. They slept among the high piles of belongings. Tijmen lay on the sofa, to which he felt he was entitled as the new 'Duke of Sapna'. But he slept badly; it was as if the spirit of the occupants was still haunting the house. For hours he listened to the explosions around the village.

They left at the crack of dawn in order to avoid the Serbs' heavy artillery. Tijmen agreed with the Swedes that they would release smoke the moment they came under fire in order to obscure the Serbs' view.

It was six in the morning. The mist had not yet completely lifted. The men were quiet. Oscar, the doc, was slumped listlessly on a seat at the back, his face still creased with sleep. Niels, two metres tall, bent double at the gun port, was sweeping the Serb bank with his machine gun. Patrick had closed the hatch and was sitting with his knees tucked up on his seat, his hand folded under his chin like a small child. There was sweat on his forehead. Milan was muttering inaudibly with a face twisted like a rubber mask being squeezed by an invisible hand.

Jacco, the driver, accelerated. Another hundred metres and the first vehicle would have reached the road. Jacco put his foot down even further. Then suddenly: the rattle of machine guns. Smoke in the verge. They ducked, even though they were in an armoured vehicle. Tijmen first closed Jacco's hatch, then his own. A few seconds' panic as he did so. On a bend the YPR almost skidded off the road. Through his periscope Tijmen saw a spurting row of bullet strikes just in front of the vehicle, the kind you saw in films. He shouted down the intercom to Jacco, 'No heavy weapons, thank God, machine guns can't hurt us.' He didn't even notice that at each bend he was giving Jacco a tap on his helmet. The right track clawed at the verge. Tap, tap. 'Left, left, for f…'s sake…' The YPR scraped the balustrade of a bridge.

The patrol thundered through Brzava, past the headquarters of the 'First Mountain Brigade', as the Muslim brigade in control of the furthest tip of the Thumb was called. Chickens flew squawking into the verge left and right, but the inhabitants kept their heads down.

Tijmen had learned that little pointers like this could mean the difference between life and death. A little further on they realised they were out of range of Serb observation. Tijmen opened the armoured hatch, and at the same time Jacco's grinning head appeared. He pushed his goggles up onto his forehead. Around his eyes his skin was snow white, the rest of his face was a black as that of a miner.

At the road-block the barrier remained closed. Heavily armed Muslim fighters barred the way. Next to the road-block was a rusty caravan. The commander appeared in the doorway and gestured excitedly to his men. Milan translated timidly that they had to go back to Brzava. They had visited Teočak without the permission of the Muslims, who were furious. The First Mountain Brigade did not tolerate the slightest flouting of its authority in the area. Larsson decided to leave seven armoured vehicles behind here and go back alone in his own vehicle. It was difficult to persuade him that a single vehicle was hopeless.

Tijmen said, 'And what if there are casualties?'

Patrick pressed firmly against the side and carefully kept Tijmen's body between himself and the enemy.

At the headquarters there was an oppressive silence. Only the high-pitched warbling of the birds could be heard. Tijmen got out and gave orders to his men to return to the road-block at the least hint of danger. The air was shimmering above the hot asphalt. As he walked to the house, they were suddenly shrouded in dust, a whistling noise in their ears. The Swedes threw themselves to the ground. Tijmen was too flabbergasted to do the same, and stayed upright, shouting, 'Let's run to the vehicles.'

His own vehicle had already left – he heard later that it had only just escaped being hit – and he sprinted over to the Swedes. Huddled in the vehicle they waited. Three more grenades landed, frighteningly close. He felt alone among the excited Swedes.

Larsson decided to honour the commander of the First Mountain Brigade with a visit after all. Inside the Muslims vented their fury. The commander asked who had given them permission to go to Teočak. The two delegations faced each other with heads down, not giving an inch. A little later through the open window they saw two more grenades land. They continued the discussion unperturbed, but drinking their coffee their hands trembled.

On the way back to the airbase no one in the vehicle spoke. They stopped at the command post of the 205th Muslim Brigade in Sapna. The commander wore a dark-blue baseball cap with the word 'captain' on it and seemed calmer than the day before. He had the determined look of a man with power, spoke more forcefully than previously and clenched his strong tanned hands.

A dish of sausage appeared on the table, large hunks of bread and bottles of rakija, as if he were trying to say that he wanted for nothing. Tuck in, he kept gesturing. The Muslim commander must have confidence in Larsson, since he did not hesitate to show him the map with his positions on it. Standing behind him, Tijmen looked too, trying to commit to memory the positions.

Larsson said in an almost relieved tone to the commander that this was the last time he would be visiting the area, and that from 11 June his duties would be taken over by Tijmen's company. The commander gave Larsson a home-made weapon, saying, 'This is what we began the war with.' He did not want to give away too much about the fighting of a day before and the bodies by the roadside, but simply muttered something about Muslims who were used as human shields.

Only when they got back to the airbase did Tijmen breathe a sigh of relief. The Swedes did not say goodbye, but raced on towards Tuzla. Speedy was already at the gate. He had followed everything on the Swedes' radio. The Jordanian radar unit was operational and had determined where the grenades had been fired from. Speedy pricked the coordinates on a map and found himself in the middle of the reservoir. 'Either the Serbs have submarines,' said Speedy, 'or it's because only two Jordanian officers were trained on American equipment. The rest had their training here.'

That evening, at the command post, Tijmen found a letter from the airbase commander. In the fading evening light he opened the envelope and read: 'The A-coy has been conducting its task in an excellent way, with a professionalism not many coys can be compared with. It's with special feelings I now thank the A-coy for an outstanding effort in securing the Airbase.'
He would read the rest later, but now he must check all observation posts and issue patrol orders for tomorrow. In the north more grenades landed and at the front-line the houses cowered lower and lower. The people in the Thumb said, 'Ten or so casualties a day,' and, 'well, you learn to live with it...'

Tijmen closed his eyes and tried hard to think of other things. In vain. The crushing silence of the flat roared in his ears. Cold sweat. No strength in arms or legs. He fell prey to his own confusion. His memories had ambushed him: the king alone with the kingdom he had dreamed. No one must come too close to him anymore. No longer dependent on anyone. It wasn't who they *thought* he was but who he *was*.

With arms folded he searched for images to hold on to. It was as if he were picked up like a rag doll and taken back to the last evening of his tour of duty. First a bird's-eye view, then closer and closer, ever closer...

It got hotter every day. The gentle spring sunshine had gone and during the day it was so searingly hot that even the shade shimmered with the garish colours of summer. On the green hills around Simin Han increasingly large yellow patches appeared.

The village was populated by hundreds of refugees, but without the dull-eyed look they seemed to have elsewhere. When a UN vehicle passed, people waved cheerfully after it.

In the midst of this Ardennes-like landscape lay the new camp, in the low-lying part of the village, on the road from Tuzla to Zvornik. There, on the edge of the Sapna Thumb, a few kilometres from Tuzla, was the base of Alpha Company.

The large asphalted vehicle park was the main reason why this spot had been chosen. The greater part of the site was taken up with the vehicle fleet, but there were also green service tents and a bunker in which the whole company could take shelter in the event of danger. White prefabs had been set up in which the soldiers slept in two long parallel rows, creating a 'street' along which the laundry of the occupants hung drying motionless in the blistering sun. It was so hot by now that all the soldiers had exchanged their heavy combat boots for much lighter ones made of khaki-coloured cotton.

Beyond the large expanse of asphalt was a field, just inside the fence, which was tended every day by an old man who had a special pass for the purpose. He was a stooped, wrinkled chap in blue overalls, who was soon a familiar figure to the company and who greeted every one he met by doffing his beret. Next to the field, close to the stream that flowed behind the camp, was an old well that had once served the distillery. Its rusty brown remnants were still visible.

The large white building, which they had found burnt out in June, had been completely refurbished, and a new corrugated metal roof had been put on it. The ground floor contained the kitchen, the mess hall and a garage where maintenance could be carried out on the vehicles. On the first floor there was a bar with a large caricature on the wall of the 'Duke of Sapna': a little chap strutting along holding a field-marshal's baton. If you looked closely you could see Tijmen's features in the face. And on the roof of this building a robust lookout post had been built, three sandbags thick, with a view of the village.

Next to the large building was a lower one, with the rooms of the company staff, administration, the command post and field hospital. On the roof was a large, resplendent red cross and next to the entrance hung a pig's head, secretly dubbed 'Frank' by the men; a gift to Speedy from the First Mountain Brigade.

When they arrived the former agricultural cooperative had looked as if no one had set foot on the site for years, but now it was buzzing with activity. A shovel loader collected sand to fill bags. Construction was still proceeding at full steam ahead at the camp and armoured vehicles came and went. The growl of the heavy diesel engines rang out across the site. Every day there were two patrols: one close by, in the relatively safe area around the village, and one that penetrated deep into the Sapna Thumb and did not return till late in the afternoon.

Every other day a supply convoy went to observation post Tango 2 with fresh water, food, fuel and ammunition – through Rainci Gornji, past the mosque with a hole right through the minaret, straight across the flat fields east of the base and quickly through Kalesija, where you came to within a thousand metres of the Serb positions. Kalesija where you passed the wall covered with the four Serb characters C. By the side of the road the dismantled houses seemed to be kneeling: a ghost town. Then into the mountains via a winding semi-hardened road, which according to the villagers had been built in 1911 by the Austro-Hungarian army, to the observation post.

The men were so keen to go to Tango 2, mostly for a week, glad as they were to have a break from tedium and the camp. The observation post was situated in a white house and reinforced on all sides with sandbags. It was sandwiched between the opposing sides and was exactly on the front-line. A hundred metres beyond, hidden from view by a pinewood, was a Muslim mortar position, and way down below, if you screwed your eyes up you could see the Serb tanks on the road from Zvornik to Tuzla.

The lynch-pin of the post was Sergeant Veldman, a born NCO, hardened by years spent with the commandos in Roosendaal. For the two months that the company occupied Tango 2 he did not want to be relieved. He was as hard as nails, but popular with the soldiers. Veldman spelt action. His speciality was 'green' sorties into no-man's-land, which meant mapping the trenches of the two sides using soldiers wearing camouflage. Tijmen found this out by chance, and immediately forbade it.

When Veldman first arrived at the post he had asked Tijmen what he thought about the fact that women were being offered by the villagers of nearby Jajici. 'It's out of the question of course,' Tijmen had said, and Veldman had fully agreed. Later the sergeant had told the men that he had tried, but that the captain refused to allow it.

The overgrown garden behind the low staff building was the only place on the whole site that had not yet been touched by the new occupants. Thistles, acanthus and weeds ran riot here. Tijmen called it his garden, and every day held his company meetings under a broad plum tree. He was sitting there now, dressed in combat trousers with a white T-shirt sporting in large letters 'Duke of Sapna Thumb'. His parents had sent it from the Netherlands at his request, as if nothing had changed inside him.

On the road past the camp, which a few kilometres further on went into no-man's-land, the occasional farm cart or lorry rattled past laden with soldiers in ash-grey uniform on their way to the front. A group of children shouted Dutch swearwords at the sentries walking past, and if the soldiers reacted they scattered amid peals of laughter.

Tijmen was looking forward to going back to the Netherlands, because since a couple of his successors had appeared the camp was every day becoming a little less the 'Home of the King's Company'. The sign with those words on it had already been removed from the main gate. The compound was now intended for others, with alien eyes and new rules.

They had built camp in less than nine weeks and there had still been no casualties, though the patrols were coming under fire more and more often. Boudewijn, the chaplain, who had joined the company just before their departure from Tuzla Airbase, had said in the Sunday service that they must be on their guard against the nonchalance that threatened to creep in.

Tuzla Airbase. That seemed a long time ago, before his leave. In mid-June, during Tijmen's holiday, Speedy had come under fire on his way to Teočak, at almost the same spot where it had previously happened to Tijmen himself. An American lady from UNICEF had been travelling with Speedy, elegant in a blue suit, with a coiffure stiff with hairspray. She had introduced herself as 'Chelsea'. As she did so she did not look at Speedy but at her own shoes. 'They're completely ruined,' she screamed. Speedy had said, 'Chelsea is a great football club'. 'But a hotel too,' retorted the woman, with a look suggesting that the American president's daughter had been named after her personally.

Once they arrived in Teočak, she immediately forgot about her shoes. She greeted everyone she met with two hands, hugged children, occasionally handed out dollars and every time she said goodbye waved by moving her fingers towards her palm, 'Have a nice day'.

She tapped some children on the cheek in farewell, as though she had landed in the jungle. Finally she had taken the local doctor to one side to discuss a very important matter with him.

In the hospital she showed him glossy posters and brochures in which mothers were exhorted in strident terms to breastfeed their babies. 'It was as if she might burst into tears at any moment,' Speedy had said. The doctor had listened calmly until she said portentously that it 'really was a matter of life and death'. At that moment the doctor interrupted her brusquely. 'I think I have better ways of spending my time,' he had said, and walked out, leaving the American woman flabbergasted.

The sound of a ball penetrated the garden. Three boys wearing baseball caps back to front were playing football on the school playground. The police chief of Simin Han was watching and laughing.

Tijmen had paid a visit to this police chief with Boudewijn. When they shook hands Tijmen had recoiled from his bad breath. A whole row of gold teeth gleamed in his mouth. The policeman had launched into an explanation of Yugoslav history. Milan, who had accompanied them from Simin Han, seeing Tijmen's boredom had only translated half of what was said. Not long afterward they started on the rakija – it was nine-thirty in the morning. He had hesitated, but Boudewijn said, 'Why not? Drink and be merry.'

'Yes,' he had answered, 'drink and be merry.'

For the rest of the day he had a dry mouth and breath that was almost as bad as the police chief's.

It was a melancholy evening, the very last shift had just returned from Tango 2. Tijmen thoughts went back to the first day in June. They had only just arrived in the new camp. The sentry at the gate had reported that the mayor and the police chief wanted to speak with the commandant. A little later they stood in front of him: a tough-looking policeman and a friendly old man, a frail figure with a deeply lined face, yellowy brown liver spots and knotty veins on his hands.

'Aristid Sarajlić,' the old man said.

Tijmen had taken the proffered hand. It felt as clammy as his own. The men got quickly to the point.

'Sandbags for the school, medicine for the hospital and repairs to the bridge in the village, perhaps you could...?'

He had dismissed the suggestion. They had drunk their coffee in silence and when the mayor looked back from the doorway, the image of that friendly old man with his hat in his hand had been etched on his mind.

Tijmen lit up his cigar. Again he heard the mayor's voice.

'Look,' he had said, 'the rest of this is in France, together with my pension, which I haven't received for the last two years.'

He showed the stump of his missing finger, and immediately afterwards came the invitation to visit him at home.

'Away from here,' Aristid had said. 'And without him,' he'd added, pointing to Milan.

The house he had later visited was at the end of a winding country road, on a hill with a panoramic view of his village: a 'French' house with thick walls, shutters, knick-knacks in the windows, and a vegetable garden at the side.

The mayor had asked about personal matters.

'Such a handsome man, and still a bachelor.'

The image of his wife, rummaging about in the kitchen. That voice again, 'But this house came close to being wiped off the map. At the beginning of the war the Serbs came very close, but fortunately they were beaten back towards Kalesija.'

With his arm the mayor gestured towards the front line. 'I still don't hate them, but I alone can't stop the war, I'm just a "small fish".'

Before Tijmen could respond, Aristid said excitedly, 'I hadn't spoken to my brother for two years, but this morning I had him on the telephone!'

Tijmen had wanted to say something nice, and muttered that the material for repairing the bridge had been arranged.

'Today you're my guest, here in the home of Aristid Sarajlić, a small fish,' replied the mayor. Tijmen had seen from his look that he should not go on about it.

Tijmen filled his glass with the wine he had saved for this last evening.

He remembered women in floral dresses dancing with little children; the local mafia boss, the owner of the only shop in Simin Han, who had given him a nod of encouragement. Only at that farewell party a few days earlier had he realised that the mayor had been his only real contact with the local population during the whole of his tour. That was also when he had been given a book on the history of Tuzla.

For a moment he saw Aristid clearly and again heard his speech at the farewell party. Then Tijmen remembered his own reply, Milan's halting translation and the offering of gifts; the children from the primary school, who had given a performance for which they had practised for weeks, their teacher who conducted from his harmonium; his men, who whistled when two twelve-year-old girls in pink suits did a dance to the music of the Bosnian entry for the Eurovision Song Contest, and how Aristid started smiling broadly; the hotel table that had, in the meantime, filled up with beer and snacks while the rest had to make do with two bottles apiece; the camera crew from Tuzla TV that suddenly turned up to film the 'fraternisation' between UNPROFOR and the Muslims – Serb grenades landed next to the camp the following day – the fat matrons who had prepared food and looked intently at his face whenever he ate a mouthful; his own unhappy expression when he had to dance with Aristid in a wide circle; the mafioso who came to his rescue and took him back to the main table and the beer; and Tijmen remembered especially the children who had peered in through chinks in the wood so as not to miss anything of the party, open-mouthed as if a circus had come to town.

Tijmen started out of his drowsy musings and shook off the memory of the farewell party. Evening fell, the light quickly faded and the last glow still lit the summit of the hills. The lights of the village gradually came on, in an overwhelming absence of sound.

He had already spent an hour alone, a rarity, when the silhouettes of the men he knew so well loomed up out of the dusk: Speedy, Herman, Boudewijn, Raymond and Oscar, the doc. They spent whole evenings after dinner around the table in his garden. He divided the wine equally among the mugs they pushed towards him and reflected that Frank was never with them anymore. He had plunged back with renewed enthusiasm into beetle collecting. Shortly before, he had presented Frank with his UN medal, given to everyone who served in Bosnia, Frank had taken it as an insult. At least, that was what he had told Boudewijn.

Speedy's voice rang through the evening air. He told them, eyes gleaming, about his leave and the way his little son had reacted when he was given his mini-Nikes. Raymond had decided to take his children to a theme park when he got back. Oscar told them about the plot he had bought – 'very cheap' – to build his new house on.

'It does look out over a cemetery, though,' he said triumphantly.

The men laughed. Herman listened in silence.

'The first thing I'm going to do when I get back,' said Boudewijn, 'is go out for a fine meal.'

'You know what my favourite meal of all is?' said Tijmen. 'Thick Belgian chips with mussels and garlic sauce, with a wheat beer.'

The food fantasies tumbled out thick and fast. Even Herman, who normally kept aloof, joined in the conversation. 'A good meal makes a new man of you,' he said, looking as if he could use some good food.

'At home I always eat healthily,' said Speedy.

There was a moment's silence, broken only by the sound of the crickets, as if they were carrying his homesickness into no-man's-land.

They went on talking for a little, until one by one they got up to go to bed.

It had taken quite a while before they had penetrated Tijmen's heart, now he was peeling away the memory of them, skin by skin. They would leave scars, the stinking wounds of lost years. He would have to go on until the last stone between inner and outer worlds was demolished.

Only Boudewijn, the chaplain, was left. They sat silently opposite each other, staring into the darkness.

'Wait,' Tijmen called out, 'I'll just go and fetch something to drink.'

He came back with a bottle of rakija and poured them a drink. Boudewijn sipped cautiously from his mug. The light of his torch on the table lit the lower part of Tijmen's face. The mosquitoes danced in the light.

'I've had it with the army,' said Tijmen suddenly. 'Christ, how I've had it.'

He looked as if it were his death sentence.

'I wouldn't shout it from the rooftops yet awhile,' said Boudewijn. 'It won't exactly win you any friends.'

If Tijmen had not been blinded by the light of the torch he would have been able to see Boudewijn's worried face.

'So you think I should keep my mouth shut?'

'That's not what I'm saying. All I'm saying is that they won't like it.'

'And you?'

'It's not about what *I* think. They'll say you've gone nuts.'

'And you won't deny that?'

'Come on,' said Boudewijn grinning, 'any fool can see what's going on. You must do as you think fit.'

'That's what I wanted to hear,' said Tijmen softly. He went on, 'Did you know I was nineteen before I knew what I wanted to do?' And without waiting for an answer, 'When I was nineteen I had a dream. But by the time I was twenty I already knew what I didn't want to be. That is, what I've become, the betrayal of my own self. I mean: the dream was smashed to smithereens.'

His speech became more and more hectic.

'Since then I've simply lived by putting things off. I thought I could beat them on their own ground. It's not true, Boudewijn. Not true. The uniform I once longed to wear now seems ridiculous to me, suffocating even. The greatest stupidity was accepting the superficiality with which I surrounded myself. I was king of that world. I seemed to be master of my own existence, but in reality I was the squanderer of my own talent, discarder of my own youth. Or is this all very confusing?'

'Very confusing,' repeated Boudewijn, looking at him with eyes full of alarm.

Tijmen got up abruptly, wished Boudewijn good night and walked towards the staff building. It wasn't what he had seen, it was what he hadn't seen; it was looking round at where he'd been. Someone had once written: 'The great art is to tell the truth by lying about it.'

It was as if the last six months were compacted together, the memories that stretched his arteries as if his head were being blown up, the glued-together fragments of his memory, the story he wanted to make into a whole; he had landed in his own story.

The warmth of the flat grabbed Tijmen by the throat. He opened the door to the balcony. With a gust of cool air sounds entered, snatches of music from the town centre. His cheeks glowed. He searched for the right words, a well-turned sentence; a single image to hold his restlessness in check. These intercepted all other thoughts. He had nothing left except his memories.

From outside came the sound of a train thundering past: the intercity train from Zwolle.

It's not what I've seen, it's what I've not seen; it's always looking round at where you've been.

The man at the road-block demands a cigarette. At home he beats his wife. Today for the first time she puts her headscarf on. She thinks of her son: her Muslim man, who works in the fields, listens intently to the sky. His father taught him that. He also learned how to kill someone who used to be your friend or neighbour and about 'Četniks', Hitler and 'Ustašas' and 'this land is mine and I'm in charge', 'I work the clay'. 'The "you lot" and "they"', 'the "we" and "them"', 'the "we know our own kind"'.

It's not what I've heard, it's what I've not heard; it's the tone of a word. The cruel mouth of the police chief bellows a lengthy story. I drink from his cup of history and sip home-distilled rakija. On the hill burnt-out men slowly demolish the scorched houses. He says, 'It's not about religion'. He says, 'My past is my fate', and that he kills with his own hands. He laughs and reveals his crooked teeth.

It's not what I do, it's what I *don't* do; it's that I'm part of it too. Down the highway from 1911 trudge silent columns of slaves with jerry-cans and wood, the wrecked signposts Teočak, Zvornik, Tuzla, Brzava, below them 'snajper' with an arrow. I wave at a black Mercedes with two skulls on the bonnet and at the sides thick steel plates. Every day I pass the mosque with the hole through the middle of the minaret. At the front, the houses hide lower and lower and in the village the clocks show a different time: they save time as a precious item, the crown jewels of a dead king. In Stari Teočak I drink Turska kava outside on the terrace. They say, 'For the first time in two years'. They speak endlessly of peace, 'but only when that house over there...'. They peer doggedly into the distance. I write home 'dobar dan' and 'kako ste', and of course all the dirty words. I write home: 'it's nice weather' and 'send me all the papers'.

It's not what I write; it's what I *don't* write. The battle subsided when the snow came, but the chimneys of hate smoked all winter long. On the first day of spring they left their houses. Their boots stamped the earth warm. The rivers melted and their cries mounted. The victorious army was welcomed by old people with children holding their hand. They whisper, 'Don't let go, because the roads are mined'. They whisper, 'Don't betray them'. They sing a children's song and the soldiers laugh.

It's not what I know, it's what I *don't* know, things whose priority seemed low. The children at the gate, who dream of Holandski bataljon, are forever crying 'sweets'. They dream of sweets and Holandija. The orchestra plays for those who want to hear... music by an unknown composer.

It's not what they hear, it's what I don't want to see, I'm thirty-two and don't want to die.

Also by Arnold Jansen op de Haar from Holland Park Press:

Yugoslav Requiem
Joegoslavisch requiem
De koning van Tuzla
Angel
Engel

THE AUTHOR

In 1994, before the fall of the Srebrenica enclave, Arnold Jansen op de Haar (born 1962) was on active service in the former Yugoslavia as the commanding officer of a UN unit. He left the Dutch Grenadier Guards in 1995 to become a full time poet and columnist and has written *Angel* (*Engel*), the sequel to *King of Tuzla* (*De koning van Tuzla*). His poetry collection *Yugoslav Requiem* (*Joegoslavisch requiem*) is a companion to King of Tuzla. He writes a weekly column for Holland Park Press' online magazine.

More details are available from
www.hollandparkpress.co.uk/jansenopdehaar

THE TRANSLATOR

Paul Vincent has been translating Dutch literature for the past twenty years, having previously taught Dutch at University College London. He was the recipient of the first David Reid Poetry Translation Prize for his translation of Hendrik Marsman's famous poem *Herinnering aan Holland* (*Memory of Holland*). He has translated the works of many leading Dutch authors, including: Louis Paul Boon, Louis Couperus, Willem Elsschot, Hans Maarten van den Brink and Harry Mulisch. For Holland Park Press, Paul Vincent also translated *Yugoslav Requiem* by Arnold Jansen op de Haar.

More details are available from
www.hollandparkpress.co.uk/translators.php

Holland Park Press is a unique publishing initiative. It gives contemporary Dutch writers the opportunity to be published in Dutch and English. We also publish new works written in English and translations of classic Dutch novels.

To
- Find out more
- Learn more about Arnold Jansen op de Haar
- Discover other interesting books
- Read our unique Anglo-Dutch magazine
- Practice your writing skills
- Take part in discussions
- Or just make a comment

Visit

www.hollandparkpress.co.uk